D0457511

DIANA PALMER

JOAN JOHNSTON

LONE STAR CHRISTMAS

Silhouette Books

Published by Silhouette Books

America's Publisher of Contemporary Romance

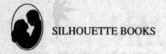

SILHOUETTE BOOKS

LONE STAR CHRISTMAS

Copyright © 1997 by Harlequin Books S.A.

ISBN 0-373-48353-8

The publisher acknowledges the copyright holders of the individual works as follows:
CHRISTMAS COWBOY
Copyright © 1997 by Diana Palmer
A HAWK'S WAY CHRISTMAS
Copyright © 1997 by Joan Mertens Johnston, Inc.

CONTENTS

DIANA PALMER:

With over 10 million copies of her books in print, bestselling, award-winning author DIANA PALMER is one of North America's most beloved authors. She got her start in writing as a newspaper reporter and published her first romance novel for Silhouette Books in 1982. In 1993 she celebrated the publication of her fiftieth novel for Silhouette Books. *Affaire de Coeur* lists her as one of the top ten romance authors in the country. Diana Palmer is the winner of numerous national Waldenbooks Romance Bestseller awards and national B. Dalton Books Bestseller awards. Her fans the world over treasure her sensual and charming stories.

Diana Palmer's next novel, *The Princess Bride,* will be published in March 1998, by Silhouette Romance. It is the first book in an exciting new promotion, VIRGIN BRIDES.

JOAN JOHNSTON:

Bestselling author Joan Johnston is the celebrated author of 35 books and novellas, which have appeared on national bestseller lists more than 50 times and have been translated into 19 languages in 25 countries worldwide. Joan writes historical and contemporary romance, and has won numerous awards for her work from the Romance Writers of America, Georgia Romance Writers and *Romantic Times* magazine.

Joan's next novel, *The Bodyguard,* will be published in March 1998. And look for another Hawk's Way novel from Silhouette Books in August.

CHRISTMAS COWBOY

Diana Palmer

To the men and women of the
Cornelia Police Department

Chapter 1

It was the holiday season in Jacobsville, Texas. Gaily colored strands of lights crisscrossed the main street, and green garlands and wreaths graced each telephone pole along the way. In the center of town, all the small maple trees that grew out of square beds at intervals along the sidewalk were decorated with lights as well.

People were bundled in coats, because even in south Texas it was cold in late November. They rushed along with shopping bags full of festively wrapped presents to go under the tree. And over on East Main Street, the Optimist Club had its yearly Christmas tree lot open already. A family of four was browsing its sawdust-covered grounds, early enough to have the pick of the beautifully shaped fir trees, just after Thanksgiving.

Dorie Wayne gazed at her surroundings the way a child would look through a store window at toys she

couldn't afford. Her hand went to the thin scar down
an otherwise perfect cheek and she shivered. How
long ago it seemed that she stood right here on this
street corner in front of the Jacobsville Drugstore, and
backed away from Corrigan Hart. It had been an in-
stinctive move; at eighteen, he'd frightened her. He
was so very masculine, a mature man with a cold
temper and an iron will. He'd set his sights on Dorie,
who found him fearful instead of attractive, despite
the fact that any single woman hereabouts would have
gone to him on her knees.

She recalled his jet black hair and pale, metallic
eyes. She'd wondered at first if it wasn't her fairness
that attracted him, because he was so dark. Dorie had
hair so blond it was almost platinum, and it was cut
short, falling into natural thick waves. Her complex-
ion was delicate and fair, and she had big gray eyes,
just a shade darker than Corrigan's. He was very
handsome—unlike his brothers. At least, that was
what people said. Dorie hadn't gotten to meet the others when she left Jacobsville. And only Corrigan and
three of his brothers lived in Jacobsville. The fifth
Hart male wasn't talked about, ever. His name wasn't
even known locally.

Corrigan and three of his four brothers had come
down to Jacobsville from San Antonio eight years ago
to take over the rich cattle operation their grandfather
had left to them in his will.

It had been something of a local joke that the Harts
had no hearts, because they seemed immune to
women. They kept to themselves and there was no
gossip about them with women. But that changed
when Dorie attended a local square dance and found

herself whirling around the floor in Corrigan Hart's arms.

Never one to pull his punches, he made his intentions obvious right at the start. He found her attractive. He was drawn to her. He wanted her. Just like that.

There was never any mention of marriage, engagement or even some furtive live-in arrangement. Corrigan said often that he wasn't the marrying kind. He didn't want ties. He made that very clear, because there was never any discussions of taking her to meet his brothers. He kept her away from their ranch.

But despite his aversion to relationships, he couldn't seem to see enough of Dorie. He wanted her and with every new kiss Dorie grew weaker and hungrier for him.

Then one spring day, he kissed her into oblivion, picked her up in his arms and carried her right into her own bedroom the minute her father left for his weekly poker game.

Despite the drugging effect of masterful kisses and the poignant trembling his expert hands aroused, Dorie had come to her senses just barely in time and pushed him away. Dazed, he'd looked down at her with stunned, puzzled eyes, only belatedly realizing that she was trying to get away, not closer.

She remembered, red-faced even now, how he'd pulled away and stood up, breathing raggedly, eyes blazing with frustrated desire. He'd treated her to a scalding lecture about girls who teased. She'd treated him to one about confirmed bachelors who wouldn't take no for an answer, especially since she'd told him she wasn't the sleep-around sort.

He didn't buy that, he'd told her coldly. She was just holding out for marriage, and there was no hope in that direction. He wanted to sleep with her, and she sure seemed to want him, too. But he didn't want her for keeps.

Dorie had been in love with him, and his emotional rejection had broken something fragile inside her. But she hadn't been about to let him see her pain.

He'd gone on, in the same vein. One insult had led to another, and once he'd gotten really worked up, he'd stormed out the door. His parting shot had been that she must be nuts if she thought he was going to buy her being a virgin. There was no such thing anymore, even at the young age of eighteen.

His rejection had closed doors between them. Dorie couldn't bear the thought of staying in Jacobsville and having everybody know that Corrigan Hart had thrown her aside because she wouldn't sleep with him. And everybody *would* know, somehow. They always knew the secret things in small towns.

That very night Dorie had made up her mind to take up her cousin Belinda's offer to come to New York and get into modeling. Certainly Dorie had the looks and figure for it. She might be young, but she had poise and grace and an exquisite face framed by short, wavy blond hair. Out of that face, huge gray eyes shone like beacons, mirroring happiness or sorrow.

After that sordid evening, Dorie cut her losses and bought a bus ticket.

She'd been standing right here, on this very corner, waiting for the bus to pick her up in front of this drugstore, when Corrigan had found her.

Her abrupt withdrawal from him had halted him in his tracks. Whatever he'd been going to say, her shamed refusal to look at him, combined with her backward steps, stopped him. She was still smarting from his angry words, as well as from her own uninhibited behavior. She was ashamed that she'd given him such license with her body now that she knew there had only been desire on his part.

He hadn't said a single word before the bus stopped for her. He hadn't said a word as she hurriedly gave her ticket to the driver, got on the bus and waited for it to leave without looking his way again. He'd stood there in the trickling rain, without even a raincoat, with his hands deep in his jean pockets, and watched the bus pull away from the curb. That was how Dorie had remembered him all the long years, a lonely fading figure in the distance.

She'd loved him desperately. But her own self-respect wouldn't let her settle for a furtive affair in the goldfish-bowl atmosphere of Jacobsville. She'd wanted a home, a husband, children, everything.

Corrigan had only wanted to sleep with her.

She'd gone, breathless and sick at heart, all the way to New York City, swearing her father to absolute secrecy about her movements.

There had been a letter, a few weeks after her arrival, from her father. In it, he told her that he'd seen Corrigan only once since her departure, and that he was now hot in pursuit of a rich divorcée with sophistication dripping from her fingers. If Dorie had any parting regrets about her decision to leave town, that was the end of them. Corrigan had made his feelings plain, if he was seeing some woman already.

Dorie wondered if her father hadn't said something unpleasant to Corrigan Hart about his daughter's sudden departure from home. It would have been like him. He was fiercely protective of his only child, especially since the death of her mother from heart disease some years past. And his opinion about philandering men was obvious to everyone.

He believed in the old-fashioned sort of courtship, the kind that ended in marriage. Only a handful of conventional people were left, he told Dorie over and over. Such people were the cornerstones of social order. If they all fell, chaos reigned. A man who loved a woman would want to give her, and his children, his name. And Corrigan, he added, had made it clear to the whole town that he wanted no part of marriage or a family. Dorie would have been asking for heartbreak if she'd given in to Corrigan's selfish demands.

Her father was dead now. Dorie had come home for the funeral as well as to dispose of the house and property and decide her own future. She'd started out with such hopes of becoming a successful model. Her eyes closed and she shivered unconsciously at the memories.

"Dorie?"

She turned at the hesitant sound of her name. The face took a little longer to recognize. "Abby?" she said. "Abby Clark!"

"Abby Ballenger," the other woman corrected with a grin. "I married Calhoun."

"Calhoun!" Dorie was momentarily floored. The younger Ballenger brother had been a rounder and a half, and he was married? And to Abby, of all people, the shy and sweet girl for whom Calhoun and Justin had shared guardianship following the death of their parents.

"Surprising, isn't it?" Abby asked, hugging the other woman. "And there's more. We have three sons."

"I haven't been away that long, have I?" Dorie asked hesitantly.

"Eight years," came the reply. Abby was a little older, but she still had the same pretty gray-blue eyes and dark hair, even if it had silver threads now. "Justin married Shelby Jacobs just after I married Calhoun. They have three sons, too," she added on a sigh. "Not a girl in the bunch."

Dorie shook her head. "For heaven's sake!"

"We heard that you were in modeling..." Her voice trailed away as she saw the obvious long scar on the once-perfect cheek. "What happened?"

Dorie's eyes were all but dead. "Not much. I decided that modeling wasn't for me." She laughed at some private joke. "I went back to school and completed a course in business. Now I work for a group of attorneys. I'm a stenographer." Her gaze fell. "Jacobsville hasn't changed a bit."

"Jacobsville never changes," Abby chuckled. "I find it comforting." The laughter went out of her eyes. "We all heard about your father. I'm sorry. It must have been a blow."

"He'd been in the nursing home near me for some time, but he always said he wanted to be buried here. That's why I brought him home. I appreciated so many people coming to the funeral. It was kind."

"I suppose you noticed one missing face in the crowd?" Abby asked carefully, because she knew how persistent Corrigan Hart had been in his pursuit of Dorie.

"Yes." She twisted her purse in her hands. "Are they still making jokes about the Hart boys?"

"More than ever. There's never been the slightest hint of gossip about any of them and a woman. I guess they're all determined to die single. Especially Corrigan. He's turned into a recluse. He stays out at the ranch all the time now. He's never seen."

"Why?"

Abby seemed evasive. "He doesn't mix and nobody knows much about his life. Odd, isn't it, in a town this small, where we mostly know each other's business, that he isn't talked about? But he stays out of sight and none of the other boys ever speak about him. He's become the original local mystery."

"Well, don't look at me as if I'm the answer. He couldn't get rid of me fast enough," she said with a twinge of remaining bitterness.

"That's what you think. He became a holy terror in the weeks after you left town. Nobody would go near him."

"He only wanted me," Dorie said doggedly.

Abby's eyes narrowed. "And you were terrified of him," she recalled. "Calhoun used to joke about it. You were such an innocent and Corrigan was a rounder. He said it was poetic justice that rakes got caught by innocents."

"I remember Calhoun being a rake."

"He was," Abby recalled. "But not now. He's reformed. He's the greatest family man I could have imagined, a doting father and a wonderful husband." She sobered. "I'm sorry things didn't work out for you and Corrigan. If you hadn't taken off like that, I think he might have decided that he couldn't live without you."

"God forbid," she laughed, her eyes quick and nervous. "He wasn't a marrying man. He said so, frequently. And I was raised…well, you know how Dad was. Ministers have a decidedly conventional outlook on life."

"I know."

"I haven't had such a bad time of it," she lied, grateful that her old friend couldn't read minds. She smiled. "I like New York."

"Do you have anyone there?"

"You mean a boyfriend, or what do they call it, a significant other?" she murmured. "No. I…don't have much to do with men."

There was a strangely haunted look about her that Abby quickly dispelled with an offer of coffee and a sandwich in the local café.

"Yes, thanks, I'm not hungry but I'd love some hot chocolate."

"Great!" Abby said. "I've got an hour to kill before I have to pick my two oldest boys up at school and the youngest from kindergarten. I'll enjoy your company."

The café was all but empty. It was a slow day, and except for a disgruntled looking cowboy sitting alone at a corner table, it was deserted.

Barbara, the owner, took their orders with a grin. "Nice to have pleasant company," she said, glaring toward the cowboy in the corner. "He brought a little black cloud in with him, and it's growing." She leaned closer. "He's one of the Hart employees," she whispered. "Or, he was until this morning. It seems that Corrigan fired him."

The sound of the man's name was enough to make Dorie's heart race, even after so many years. But she steeled herself not to let it show. She had nothing left to offer Corrigan, even if he was still interested in her. And that was a laugh. If he'd cared even a little, he'd have come to New York looking for her all those years ago.

"Fired him?" Abby glanced at the man and scowled. "But that's Buck Wyley," she protested. "He's the Harts' foreman. He's been with them since they came here."

"He made a remark Corrigan didn't like. He got knocked on his pants for his trouble and summarily fired." Barbara shrugged. "The Harts are all high-tempered, but until now I always thought Corrigan was fair. What sort of boss fires a man with Christmas only three weeks away?"

"Ebenezer Scrooge?" Abby ventured dryly.

"Buck said he cut another cowboy's wages to the bone for leaving a gate open." She shook her head. "Funny, we've heard almost nothing about Corrigan for years, and all of a sudden he comes back into the light like a smoldering madman."

"So I noticed," Abby said.

Barbara wiped her hands on a dishcloth. "I don't know what happened to set him off after so many years. The other brothers have been more visible lately, but not Corrigan. I'd wondered if he'd moved away for a while. Nobody even spoke of him." She glanced at Dorie with curious eyes. "You're Dorothy

Wayne, aren't you?'' she asked then, smiling. "I thought I recognized you. Sorry about your pa.''

"Thanks,'' Dorie said automatically. She noticed how Barbara's eyes went to the thin scar on her cheek and flitted quickly away.

"I'll get your order.''

Barbara went back behind the counter and Abby's puzzled gaze went to the corner.

"Having a bad day, Buck?'' she called.

He sipped black coffee. "It couldn't get much worse, Mrs. Ballenger,'' he replied in a deep, pleasant tone. "I don't suppose Calhoun and Justin are hiring out at the feedlot?''

"They'd hire you in a minute, and you know it,'' Abby told him. She smiled. "Why don't you go out there and…''

"Oh, the devil!'' Buck muttered, his black eyes flashing. He got to his feet and stood there, vibrating, as a tall, lean figure came through the open door.

Dorie actually caught her breath. The tall man was familiar to her, even after all those years. Dressed in tight jeans, with hand-tooled boots and a chambray shirt and a neat, spotless white Stetson atop his black hair, he looked formidable, even with the cane he was using for support.

He didn't look at the table where Dorie was sitting, which was on the other side of the café from Buck.

"You fired me,'' Buck snapped at him. "What do you want, another punch at me? This time, you'll get it back in spades, gimpy leg or not!''

Corrigan Hart just stared at the man, his pale eyes like chrome sparkling in sunlight.

"Those purebred Angus we got from Montana are

coming in by truck this morning,'' he said. ''You're the only one who knows how to use the master program for the computerized herd records.''

''And you need me,'' Buck agreed with a cold smile. ''For how long?''

''Two weeks,'' came the curt reply. ''You'll work that long for your severance pay. If you're still of a mind to quit.''

''Quit, hell!'' Buck shot back, astonished. ''You fired me!''

''I did not!'' the older man replied curtly. ''I said you could mind your own damned business or get out.''

Buck's head turned and he stared at the other man for a minute. ''If I come back, you'd better keep your fists to yourself from now on,'' he said shortly.

The other man didn't blink. ''You know why you got hit.''

Buck glanced warily toward Dorie and a ruddy color ran along his high cheekbones. ''I never meant it the way you took it,'' he retorted.

''You'll think twice before you presume to make such remarks to me again, then, won't you?''

Buck made a movement that his employer took for assent.

''And your Christmas bonus is now history!'' he added.

Buck let out an angry breath, almost spoke, but crushed his lips together finally in furious submission.

''Go home!'' the older man said abruptly.

Buck pulled his hat over his eyes, tossed a dollar bill on the table with his coffee cup and strode out with barely a tip of the hat to the women present, muttering under his breath as he went.

The door closed with a snap. Corrigan Hart didn't move. He stood very still for a moment, as if steeling himself.

Then he turned, and his pale eyes stared right into Dorie's. But the anger in them eclipsed into a look of such shock that Dorie blinked.

"What happened to you?" he asked shortly.

She knew what he meant without asking. She put a hand self-consciously to her cheek. "An accident," she said stiffly.

His chin lifted. The tension in the café was so thick that Abby shifted uncomfortably at the table.

"You don't model now," he continued.

The certainty in the statement made her miserable. "No. Of course I don't."

He leaned heavily on the cane. "Sorry about your father," he said curtly.

She nodded.

His face seemed pinched as he stared at her. Even across the room, the heat in the look was tangible to Dorie. Her hands holding the mug of hot chocolate went white at the knuckles from the pressure of them around it.

He glanced at Abby. "How are things at the feed-lot?"

"Much as usual," she replied pleasantly. "Calhoun and Justin are still turning away business. Nice, in the flat cattle market this fall."

"I agree. We've culled as many head as possible and we're venturing into new areas of crossbreeding.

Nothing but purebreds now. We're hoping to pioneer a new breed.''

"Good for you," Abby replied.

His eyes went back to Dorie. They lingered on her wan face, her lack of spirit. "How long are you going to stay?" he asked.

The question was voiced in such a way it seemed like a challenge. Her shoulders rose and fell. "Until I tie up all the loose ends, I suppose. They've given me two weeks off at the law firm where I work."

"As an attorney?"

She shook her head. "A stenographer."

He scowled. "With your head for figures?" he asked shortly.

Her gaze was puzzled. She hadn't realized that he was aware of her aptitude for math.

"It's a waste," he persisted. "You'd have been a natural at bookkeeping and marketing."

She'd often thought so, too, but she hadn't pursued her interest in that field. Especially after her first attempt at modeling.

He gave her a calculating stare. "Clarisse Marston has opened a boutique in town. She designs women's clothes and has them made up at a local textile plant. She sells all over the state."

"Yes," Abby added. "In fact, she's now doing a lot of designing for Todd Burke's wife, Jane—you know, her signature rodeo line of sportswear."

"I've heard of it, even in New York," Dorie admitted.

"The thing Clarisse doesn't have is someone to help her with marketing and bookkeeping." He shook his head. "It amazes me that she hasn't gone belly-up already."

Abby started to speak, but the look on Corrigan's face silenced her. She only smiled at Dorie.

"This is your home," Corrigan persisted quietly. "You were born and raised in Jacobsville. Surely having a good job here would be preferable to being a stenographer in New York. Unless," he added slowly, "there's some reason you want to stay there."

His eyes were flashing. Dorie looked into the film on her cooling hot chocolate. "I don't have anyone in New York." She shifted her legs. "I don't have anyone here, either, now."

"But you do," Abby protested. "All your friends."

"Of course, she may miss the bright lights and excitement," Corrigan drawled.

She looked at him curiously. He was trying to goad her. Why?

"Is Jacobsville too small for you now, city girl?" he persisted with a mocking smile.

"No, it isn't that at all," she said. She cleared her throat.

"Come home," Abby coaxed.

She didn't answer.

"Still afraid of me?" Corrigan asked with a harsh laugh when her head jerked up. "That's why you left. Is it why you won't come back?"

She colored furiously, the first trace of color that had shown in her face since the strange conversation began.

"I'm not...afraid of you!" she faltered.

But she was, and he knew it. His silver eyes narrowed and that familiar, mocking smile turned up his thin upper lip. "Prove it."

"Maybe Miss Marston doesn't want a book-keeper."

"She does," he returned.

She hesitated. "She might not like me."

"She will."

She let out an exasperated sigh. "I can't make a decision that important in a few seconds," she told him. "I have to think about it."

"Take your time," he replied. "Nobody's rushing you."

"It would be lovely if you came back, though," Abby said with a smile. "No matter how many friends we have, we can always use one more."

"Exactly," Corrigan told her. His eyes narrowed. "Of course, you needn't consider me in your decision. I'm not trying to get you to come back for my sake. But I'm sure there are plenty of other bachelors left around here who'd be delighted to give you a whirl, if you needed an incentive."

His lean face was so hard and closed that not one flicker of emotion got away from it.

Abby was eyeing him curiously, but she didn't say a word, not even when her gaze fell to his hand on the silver knob of the cane and saw it go white from the pressure.

He eased up on the handle, just the same. "Well?"

"I'd like to," Dorie said quietly. She didn't look at him. Odd, how his statement had hurt, after all those years. She looked back on the past with desperation these days, wondering how her life would have been if she hadn't resisted him that night he'd tried to carry her to bed.

She hadn't wanted an affair, but he was an honorable man, in his fashion. Perhaps he would have followed up with a proposal, despite his obvious distaste for the married state. Or perhaps he wouldn't have. There might have been a child...

She grimaced and lifted the cup of chocolate to her lips. It was tepid and vaguely distasteful.

"Go see Clarisse, why don't you?" he added. "You've nothing to lose, and a lot to gain. She's a sweet woman. You'll like her."

Did he? She didn't dare wonder about that, or voice her curiosity. "I might do that," she replied.

The tap of the cane seemed unusually loud as he turned back to the door. "Give the brothers my best," Corrigan told Abby. He nodded and was gone.

Only then did Dorie look up, her eyes on his tall, muscular body as he walked carefully back to the big double-cabbed black ranch pickup truck he drove.

"What happened to him?" Dorie asked.

Abby sipped her own hot chocolate before she answered. "It happened the week after you left town. He went on a hunting trip in Montana with some other men. During a heavy, late spring snow, Corrigan and another man went off on their own in a four-wheel-drive utility vehicle to scout another section of the hunting range."

"And?" Dorie prompted.

"The truck went over a steep incline and overturned. The other man was killed outright. Corrigan was pinned and couldn't get free. He lay there most of the night and into the next day before the party came looking for them and found him. By that time, he was unconscious. The impact broke his leg in two places, and he had frostbite as well. He almost died.''

Dorie caught her breath. ''How horrible!''

''They wanted to amputate the leg, but...'' she shrugged. ''He refused them permission to operate, so they did the best they could. The leg is usable, just, but it will always be stiff. They said later that it was a miracle he didn't lose any toes. He had just enough sense left to wrap himself in one of those thin thermal sheets the men had carried on the trip. It saved him from a dangerous frostbite.''

''Poor man.''

''Oh, don't make that mistake,'' Abby mused. ''Nobody is allowed to pity Corrigan Hart. Just ask his brothers.''

''All the same, he never seemed the sort of man to lose control of anything, not even a truck.''

''He wasn't himself but he didn't lose control, either.''

''I beg your pardon?''

Abby grimaced. ''He and the other man, the one who was driving, had been drinking. He blamed himself not only for the wreck, but for the other man's death. He knew the man wasn't fit to drive but he didn't try to stop him. They say he's been punishing himself ever since. That's why he never comes into town, or has any social life. He's withdrawn into himself and nobody can drag him back out. He's become a hermit.''

''But, why?''

''Why was he drinking, you mean?'' Abby said,

and Dorie nodded. Still, Abby hesitated to put it into words.

"Tell me," came the persistent nudge from Dorie.

Abby's eyes were apologetic. "Nobody knows, really. But the gossip was that he was trying to get over losing you."

Chapter 2

"But he wanted to lose me," Dorie exclaimed, shocked. "He couldn't get out of my house fast enough when I refused...refused him," she blurted. She clasped her hands together. "He accused me of being frigid and a tease..."

"Corrigan was a rounder, Dorie," Abby said gently. "In this modern age, even in Jacobsville, a lot of girls are pretty sophisticated at eighteen. He wouldn't have known about your father being a minister, because he'd retired from the church before the Harts came to take over their grandfather's ranch. He was probably surprised to find you less accommodating than other girls."

"Surprised wasn't the word," Dorie said miserably. "He was furious."

"He did go to the bus depot when you left."

"How did you know that?"

"Everybody talked about it," Abby admitted. "It was generally thought that he went there to stop you."

"He didn't say a word," came the quiet reply. "Not one word."

"Maybe he didn't know what to say. He was probably embarrassed and upset about the way he'd treated you. A man like that might not know what to do with an innocent girl."

Dorie laughed bitterly. "Sure he did. You see her off and hope she won't come back. He told me that he had no intention of marrying."

"He could have changed his mind."

Dorie shook her head. "Not a chance. He never talked about us being a couple. He kept reminding me that I was young and that he liked variety. He said that we shouldn't think of each other in any serious way, but just enjoy each other while it lasted."

"That sounds like a Hart, all right," Abby had to admit. "They're all like Corrigan. Apparently they have a collective bad attitude toward women and think of them as minor amusements."

"He picked on the wrong girl," Dorie said. She finished her hot chocolate. "I'd never even had a real boyfriend when he came along. He was so forceful and demanding and inflexible, so devoid of tenderness when he was with me." She huddled closer into her sweater. "He came at me like a rocket. I couldn't run, I couldn't hide, he just kept coming." Her eyes closed on a long sigh. "Oh, Abby, he scared me to death. I'd been raised in a such a way that I couldn't have an affair, and I knew that was all he wanted. I ran, and kept running. Now I can't stop."

"You could, if you wanted to."

"The only way I'd come back is with a written guarantee that he wanted nothing more to do with me," she said with a cold laugh. "Otherwise, I'd never feel safe here."

"He just told you himself that he had no designs on you," Abby reminded her. "He has other interests."

"Does he? Other…women interests?"

Abby clasped her fingers together on the table. "He goes out with a rich divorcée when he's in need of company," she said. "That's been going on for a long time now. He probably was telling the truth when he said that he wouldn't bother you. After all, it's been eight years." She studied the other woman. "You want to come home, don't you?"

Caught off guard, Dorie nodded. "I'm so alone," she confessed. "I have bolts and chains on my door and I live like a prisoner when I'm not at work. I rarely ever go outside. I miss trees and green grass."

"There's always Central Park."

"You can't plant flowers there," she said, "or have a dog or cat in a tiny apartment like mine. I want to sit out in the rain and watch the stars at night. I've dreamed of coming home."

"Why haven't you?"

"Because of the way I left," she confessed. "I didn't want any more trouble than I'd already had. It was bad enough that Dad had to come and see me, that I couldn't come home."

"Because of Corrigan?"

"What?" For an instant, Dorie's eyes were frightened. Then they seemed to calm. "No, it was for another reason altogether, those first few years. I couldn't risk coming here, where it's so easy to find people..." She closed up when she realized what she was saying. "It was a problem I had, in New York. That's all I can tell you. And it's over now. There's no more danger from that direction. I'm safe."

"I don't understand."

"You don't need to know," Dorie said gently. "It wouldn't help matters to talk about it now. But I would like to come back home. I seem to have spent most of my life on the run."

What an odd turn of phrase, Abby thought, but she didn't question it. She just smiled. "Well, if you decide to come back, I'll introduce you to Clarisse. Just let me know."

Dorie brightened. "All right. Let me think about it for a day or two, and I'll be in touch with you."

"Good. I'll hold you to that."

For the next two days, Dorie thought about nothing else except coming back to her hometown. While she thought, she wandered around the small yard, looking at the empty bird feeders and the squirrel feeder nearby. She saw the discarded watering pot, the weed-bound flower beds. Her father's long absence had made its mark on the little property. It needed a loving hand to restore it.

She stood very still as an idea formed in her mind. She didn't have to sell the property. She could keep it. She could live here. With her math skills, and the bookkeeping training she'd had in business school, she could open a small bookkeeping service of her own. Clarisse could be a client. She could have others. She could support herself. She could leave New York.

The idea took wing. She was so excited about it that she called Abby the next morning when she was sure that the boys would be in school.

She outlined the idea to her friend. "Well, what do you think?" she asked enthusiastically.

"I think it's a great idea!" Abby exclaimed. "And the perfect solution. When are you going to start?"

"Next week," she said with absolute certainty. "I'll use the Christmas vacation I would have had as my notice. It will only take a couple of days to pack up the few things I have. I'll have to pay the rent, because I signed a lease, but if things work out as I hope they will, that won't be a problem. Oh, Abby, it's like a dream!"

"Now you sound more like the Dorothy I used to know," Abby told her. "I'm so glad you're coming home."

"So am I," Dorie replied, and even as she said it, she tried not to think of the complications that could arise. Corrigan was still around. But he'd made her a promise of sorts, and perhaps he'd keep it. Anyway, she'd worry about that situation later.

A week later, Dorie was settled into her father's house, with all her bittersweet memories of him to keep her company. She'd shipped her few big things, like her piano, home by a moving service. Boxes still cluttered the den, but she was beginning to get her house into some sort of order.

It needed a new roof, and some paint, as well as some plumbing work on the leaky bathtub faucet. But

those were minor inconveniences. She had a good little nest egg in her savings account and it would tide
her over, if she was careful, until she could be self-
supporting in her business again.

She had some cards and stationery printed and put
an ad in the Jacobsville weekly newspaper. Then she
settled in and began to work in the yard, despite the
cold weather. She was finding that grief had to be
worked through. It didn't end at the funeral. And the
house was a constant reminder of the old days when
she and her father had been happy.

So it was a shock to find Corrigan Hart on her
doorstep the first Saturday she was in residence.

She just stared at him at first, as if she'd been
stunned. In fact, she was. He was the last person she'd
have expected to find on her doorstep.

He had a bouquet of flowers in the hand that wasn't
holding the cane and his hat. He proferred them
brusquely.

"Housewarming present," he said.

She took the pretty bouquet and belatedly stood
aside. "Would you like to come in? I could make
coffee."

He accepted the invitation, placing his hat on the
rack by the door. He kept the cane and she noticed
that he leaned on it heavily as he made his way to
the nearest easy chair and sat down in it.

"They say damp weather is hard on injured
joints," she remarked.

His pale eyes speared into her face, with an equal
mixture of curiosity and irritation. "They're right,"
he drawled. "Walking hurts. Does it help to have me
admit it?"

"I wasn't trying to score points," she replied quietly. "I didn't get to say so in the café, but I'm sorry you got hurt."

His own eyes were pointed on the scar that ran the length of her cheek. "I'm sorry you did," he said gruffly. "You mentioned coffee?"

There it was again, that bluntness that had frightened her so much at eighteen. Despite the eight years in between, he still intimidated her.

She moved into the small kitchen, visible from the living room, and filled the pot with water and a premeasured coffee packet. After she'd started it dripping, and had laid a tray with cups, saucers and the condiments, she rejoined him.

"Are you settling in?" he asked a minute after she'd dropped down onto the sofa.

"Yes," she said. "It's strange, after being away for so many years. And I miss Dad. But I always loved this house. Eventually it will be comforting to live here. Once I get over the worst of the grieving."

He nodded. "We lost both our parents at once, in a flood," he said tersely. "I remember how we felt."

He looked around at the high ceilings and marked walls, and the open fireplace. He nodded toward it. "That isn't efficient. You need a stove in here."

"I need a lot of things in here, but I have to eat, too," she said with a faint smile. She pushed back her short, wavy platinum hair and curled up on the sofa in her jeans and gray sweatshirt and socks. Her shoes were under the sofa. Even in cold weather, she hated wearing shoes around the house.

He seemed to notice that and found it amusing, judging by the twinkle in his pale eyes.

"I hate shoes," she said.

"I remember."

That was surprising. She hardly remembered the girl she'd been eight years ago. It seemed like a lifetime.

"You had a dog, that damned little spaniel, and you were out in the front yard washing him one day when I drove by," he recalled. "He didn't like a bath, and you were soaked, bare feet, cutoffs, tank top and all." His eyes darkened as he looked at her. "I told you to go in the house, do you remember?"

"Yes." The short command had always puzzled her, because he'd seemed angry, not amused as he did now.

"I never said why," he continued. His face tautened as he looked at her. "You weren't wearing anything under that tank top and it was plastered to you," he added quietly. "You can't imagine what it did to me... And there was that damned Bobby Harris standing on the sidewalk gawking at you."

Bobby had asked her out later that day, and she'd refused, because she didn't like him. He was an older boy; her father never had liked him.

"I didn't realize," she said, amazed that the memory should be so tame now, when his odd behavior had actually hurt in the past. She actually flushed at the thought that he'd seen her that way so early in their relationship.

"I know that, now, eight years too late," he said abruptly.

She cocked her head, studying him curiously.

He saw her gaze and lifted his eyes. "I thought you were displaying your charms brazenly for my benefit, and maybe even for Bobby's," he said with a mocking smile. "That's why I acted the way I did that last night we dated."

Her face thinned with distress. "Oh, no!"

"Oh, yes," he said, his voice deep with bitterness. "I thought you were playing me for a sucker, Dorie. That you were pretending to be innocent because I was rich and you wanted a wedding ring instead of an affair."

The horror she felt showed in her wan face.

"Yes, I know," he said when she started to protest. "I only saw what I wanted to see. But the joke was on me. By the time I realized what a hell of a mistake I'd made about you, you were halfway on a bus out of town. I went after you. But I couldn't manage the right words to stop you. My pride cut my throat. I was never that wrong about anyone before."

She averted her gaze. "It was a long time ago. I was just a kid."

"Yes. Just a kid. And I mistook you for a woman." He studied her through narrow lids. "You don't look much older even now. How did you get that scar?"

Her fingers went to it. The memories poured over her, hot and hurting. She got to her feet. "I'll see about the coffee."

She heard a rough sound behind her, but apparently it wasn't something he wanted to put words to. She escaped into the kitchen, found some cookies to put in a bowl and carried the coffee back to the coffee table on a silver tray.

"Fancy stuff," he mused.

She knew that he had equally fancy stuff at his place. She'd never been there, but she'd certainly heard about the Hart heirlooms that the four brothers displayed with such pride. Old Spanish silver, five generations old, dating all the way back to Spain graced their side table. There was crystal as well, and dozens of other heirlooms that would probably never be handed down. None of the Harts, it was rumored, had any ambitions of marrying.

"This was my grandmother's," she said. "It's all I had of her. She brought this service over from England, they said."

"Ours came from Spain." He waited for her to pour the coffee. He picked up his cup, waving away cream and sugar. He took a sip, nodded and took another. "You make good coffee. Amazing how many people can't."

"I'm sure it's bad for us. Most things are."

He agreed. He put the cup back into the saucer and studied her over its rim. "Are you planning to stay for good?"

"I guess so," she faltered. "I've had stationery and cards printed, and I've already had two offers of work."

"I'm bringing you a third—our household accounts. We've been sharing them since our mother died. Consequently each of us insists that it's not our turn to do them, so they don't get done."

"You'd bring them to me?" she asked hesitantly.

He studied her broodingly. "Why shouldn't I? Are you afraid to come out to the ranch and do them?"

"Of course not."

"Of course not," he muttered, glaring at her. He sat forward, watching her uneasy movement. "Eight years, and I still frighten you."

She curled up even more. "Don't be absurd. I'm twenty-six."

"You don't look or act it."

"Go ahead," she invited. "Be as blunt as you like."

"Thanks, I will. You're still a virgin."

Coffee went everywhere. She cursed roundly, amusing him, as she searched for napkins to mop up the spill, which was mostly on her.

"Why are you?" he persisted, baiting her. "Were you waiting for me?"

She stood up, slamming the coffee cup to the floor. It shattered with a pleasantly loud crash, and she thanked goodness that it was an old one. "You son of a…!"

He stood up, too, chuckling. "That's better," he mused, watching her eyes flash, her face burn with color.

She kicked at a pottery shard. "Damn you, Corrigan Hart!"

He moved closer, watching her eyelids flutter. She tried to back up, but she couldn't go far. Her legs were against the sofa. There was no place to run.

He paused a step away from her, close enough that she could actually feel the heat of his body through her clothing and his. He looked down into her eyes without speaking for several long seconds.

"You're not the child you used to be," he said, his voice as smooth as velvet. "You can stand up for yourself, even with me. And everything's going to be all right. You're home. You're safe."

It was almost as if he knew what she'd been through. His eyes were quiet and full of secrets, but he smiled. His hand reached out and touched her short hair.

"You still wear it like a boy's," he murmured. "But it's silky. Just the way I remember it."

He was much too close. He made her nervous. Her hands went out and pressed into his shirtfront, but instead of moving back, he moved forward. She shivered at the feel of his chest under her hands, even with the shirt covering it.

"I don't want a lover," she said, almost choking on the words.

"Neither do I," he replied heavily. "So we'll be friends. That's all."

She nibbled on her lower lip. He smelled of spice and leather. She used to dream about him when she first left home. Over the years, he'd assumed the image of a protector in her mind. Strange, when he'd once frightened her so much.

Impulsively she laid her cheek against his chest with a little sigh and closed her eyes.

He shivered for an instant, before his lean hands pressed her gently to him, in a nonthreatening way. He stared over her head with eyes that blazed, eyes that he was thankful she couldn't see.

"We've lost years," he said half under his breath. "But Christmas brings miracles. Maybe we'll have one of our own."

"A miracle?" she mused, smiling. She felt ever so safe in his arms. "What sort?"

"I don't know," he murmured, absently stroking her hair. "We'll have to wait and see. You aren't going to sleep, are you?"

"Not quite." She lifted her head and looked up at

him, a little puzzled at the familiarity she felt with him. "I didn't expect that you'd ever be comfortable to be around."

"How so?"

She shrugged. "I wasn't afraid."

"Why should you be?" he replied. "We're different people now."

"I guess."

He brushed a stray hair from her eyebrow with a lean, sure hand. "I want you to know something," he said quietly. "What happened that night...I wouldn't have forced you. Things got a little out of hand, and I said some things, a lot of things, that I regret. I guess you realize now that I had a different picture of you than the one that was real. But even so, I wouldn't have harmed you."

"I think I knew that," she said. "But thank you for telling me."

His hand lay alongside her soft cheek and his metallic eyes went dark and sad. "I mourned you," he said huskily. "Nothing was the same after you'd gone."

She lowered her eyes to his throat. "I didn't have much fun in New York at first, either."

"Modeling wasn't all it was cracked up to be?"

She hesitated. Then she shook her head. "I did better as a stenographer."

"And you'll do even better as a financial expert, right here," he told her. He smiled, tilting up her chin. "Are you going to take the job I've offered you?"

"Yes," she said at once. Her gaze drew slowly over his face. "Are your brothers like you?"

"Wait and see."

"That sounds ominous."

He chuckled, moving slowly away from her to retrieve his cane from the chair. "They're no worse, at least."

"Are they as outspoken as you?"

"Definitely." He saw her apprehension. "Think of the positive side. At least you'll always know exactly where you stand with us."

"That must be a plus."

"Around here, it is. We're hard cases. We don't make friends easily."

"And you don't marry. I remember."

His face went hard. "You have plenty of reason to remember that I said that. But I'm eight years older, and a lot wiser. I don't have such concrete ideas anymore."

"You mean, you're not still a confirmed bachelor?" She laughed nervously. "They say you're taken with the gay divorcée, just the same."

"How did you hear about her?" he asked curtly.

His level, challenging gaze made her uneasy. "People talk," she said.

"Well, the gay divorcée," he emphasized, his expression becoming even more remote, "is a special case. And we're not a couple. Despite what you may have heard. We're friends."

She turned away. "That's no concern of mine. I'll do your bookkeeping on those household accounts, and thank you for the work. But I have no interest in your private life."

He didn't return the compliment. He reached for his hat and perched it on his black hair. There were threads of gray at his temples now, and new lines in his dark, lean face.

"I'm sorry about your accident," she said abruptly, watching him lean heavily on the cane.

"I'll get by," he said. "My leg is stiff, but I'm not crippled. It hurts right now because I took a toss off a horse, and I need the cane. As a rule, I walk well enough without one."

"I remember the way you used to ride," she recalled. "I thought I'd never seen anything in my life as beautiful as you astride a horse at a fast gallop."

His posture went even more rigid. "You never said so."

She smiled. "You intimidated me. I was afraid of you. And not only because you wanted me." She averted her eyes. "I wanted you, too. But I hadn't been raised to believe in a promiscuous life-style. Which," she added, looking up at his shocked face, "was all you were offering me. You said so."

"God help me, I never knew that your father was a minister and your mother a missionary," he said heavily. "Not until it was far too late to do me any good. I expected that all young women were free with their favors in this age of no-consequences intimacy."

"It wouldn't be of no consequence to me," she said firmly. "I was never one to go with the crowd. I'm still not."

"Yes, I know," he murmured dryly, giving her a long, meaningful glance. "It's obvious."

"And it's none of your business."

"I wouldn't go that far." He tilted his hat over his eyes. "I haven't changed completely, you know. I still go after the things I want, even if I don't go as fast as I used to.''

''I expect you do,'' she said. ''Does the divorcée know?''

''Know what? That I'm persistent? Sure she does.''

''Good for her.''

''She's a beauty,'' he added, propping on his stick. ''Of an age to be sophisticated and good fun.''

Her heart hurt. ''I'm sure you enjoy her company.''

''I enjoy yours as much,'' he replied surprisingly. ''Thanks for the coffee.''

''Don't you like cookies?'' she asked, noting that he hadn't touched them.

''No,'' he said. ''I don't care for sweets at all.''

''Really?''

He shrugged. ''We never had them at home. Our mother wasn't the homey sort.''

''What was she like?'' she had to ask.

''She couldn't cook, hated housework and spouted contempt for any woman who could sew and knit and crochet,'' he replied.

She felt cold. ''And your father?''

''He was a good man, but he couldn't cope with us alone.'' His eyes grew dark. ''When she took off and deserted him, part of him died. She'd just come back, out of money and all alone, from her latest lover. They were talking about a reconciliation when the flood took the house where she was living right out from under them.'' His face changed, hardened. He leaned heavily on the cane. ''Simon and Cag and I were grown by then. We took care of the other two.''

"No wonder you don't like women," she murmured quietly.

He gave her a long, level look and then dropped his gaze. She missed the calculation in his tone when he added, "Marriage is old-fashioned, anyway. I have a dog, a good horse and a houseful of modern appliances. I even have a housekeeper who can cook. A wife would be redundant."

"Well, I never," she exclaimed, breathless.

"I know," he replied, and there was suddenly a wicked glint in his eyes. "You can't blame that on me," he added. "God knows, I did my best to bring you into the age of enlightenment."

While she was absorbing that dry remark, he tipped his hat, turned and walked out the door.

She darted onto the porch after him. "When?" she called after him. "You didn't say when you wanted me to start."

"I'll phone you." He didn't look back. He got into his truck laboriously and drove away without even a wave of his hand.

At least she had the promise of a job, she told herself. She shouldn't read hidden messages into what he said. But the past he'd shared with her, about his mother, left her chilled. How could a woman have five sons and leave them?

And what was the secret about the fifth brother, Simon, the one nobody had ever seen? She wondered if he'd done something unspeakable, or if he was in trouble with the law. There had to be a reason why the brothers never spoke of him much. Perhaps she'd find out one day.

Chapter 3

It was the next day before she realized she hadn't thanked Corrigan for the flowers he'd brought. She sent a note out to the ranch on Monday, and got one back that read, simply, "You're welcome." So much for olive branches, if one had been needed.

She found plenty to keep her busy in the days that followed. It seemed that all her father's friends and the people she'd gone to school with wanted her to come home. Everyone seemed to know a potential client. It wasn't long before she was up to her ears in work.

The biggest surprise came Thursday morning when she heard the sound of many heavy footsteps and looked up from her desk to find three huge, intimidating men standing on her porch just beyond the glass-fronted door. They'd come in that big double-cabbed pickup that Corrigan usually drove, and she wondered if these were his brothers.

She went to open the door and felt like a midget when they came tromping inside her house, their spurs jingling pleasantly on boots that looked as if they'd been kept in a swamp.

"We're the Harts," one of them said. "Corrigan's brothers."

As she'd guessed. She studied them curiously. Corrigan was tall, but these men were giants. Two were dark-haired like Corrigan, and one had blond-streaked brown hair. All were dark-eyed, unlike him. None of them would have made any lists of handsome bachelors. They were rugged-looking, lean and tanned, and they made her nervous. The Hart boys made most people nervous. The only other local family that had come close to their reputations for fiery tempers were the Tremayne boys, who were all married and just a little tamer now. The Harts were relative newcomers in Jacobsville, having only been around eight years or so. But they kept to themselves and seemed to have ties to San Antonio that were hard to break. What little socializing they did was all done there, in the city. They didn't mix much in Jacobsville.

Not only were they too rugged for words, but they also had the most unusual first names Dorie could remember hearing. They introduced themselves abruptly, without even being asked first.

Reynard was the youngest. They called him Rey. He had deep-set black eyes and a thin mouth and, gossip said, the worst temper of the four.

The second youngest was Leopold. He was broader than the other three, although not fat, and the tallest. He never seemed to shave. He had blond-streaked brown hair and brown eyes and a mischievous streak that the others apparently lacked.

Callaghan was the eldest, two years older than Corrigan. He had black eyes like a cobra. He didn't blink. He was taller than all his brothers, with the exception of Leopold, and he did most of the bronc-breaking at the ranch. He looked Spanish, more than the others, and he had the bearing and arrogance of royalty, as if he belonged in another century. They said he had the old-fashioned attitudes of the past, as well.

He gave the broader of the three a push toward Dorie. He glared over his shoulder, but took off his hat and forced a smile as he stood in front of Dorie.

"You must be Dorothy Wayne," Leopold said with a grin. "You work for us."

"Y...yes, I guess I do," she stammered. She felt surrounded. She moved back behind the desk and just stared at them, feeling nervous and inadequate.

"Will you two stop glaring?" Leopold shot at his taciturn brothers. "You're scaring her!"

They seemed to make an effort to relax, although it didn't quite work out.

"Never mind," Leopold muttered. He clutched his hat in his hand. "We'd like you to come out to the ranch," he said. "The household accounts are about to do us in. We can't keep Corrigan still long enough to get him to bring them to you."

"He came over Saturday," she said.

"Yeah, we heard," Leo mused. "Roses, wasn't it?"

The other two almost smiled.

"Roses," she agreed. Her gray eyes were wide and they darted from one giant to another.

"He forgot to bring you the books. The office is in a hel...heck of a mess," Leo continued. "We can't make heads nor tails of it. Corrigan scribbles, and we've volunteered him to do it mostly, but we can't read his writing. He escaped to a herd sale in Montana, so we're stuck." He shrugged and managed to look helpless. "We can't see if we've got enough money in the account to buy groceries." He looked hungry. He sighed loudly. "We'd sure appreciate it if you could come out, maybe in the morning, about nine? If that's not too early."

"Oh, no," she said. "I'm up and making breakfast by six."

"Making breakfast? You can cook, then?" Leopold asked.

"Well, yes." She hesitated, but he looked really interested. "I make biscuits and bacon and eggs."

"Pig meat," the one called Reynard muttered.

"Steak's better," Callaghan agreed.

"If she can make biscuits, the other stuff doesn't matter," Reynard retorted.

"Will you two shut up?" Leopold asked sharply. He turned back to Dorie and gave her a thorough appraisal, although not in the least sexual. "You don't look like a bookkeeper."

"Nice hair," Reynard remarked.

"Bad scar on that cheek," Callaghan remarked. "How did it happen?"

Heavens, he was blunt! She was almost startled enough to tell him. She blurted that it had been in an accident.

"Tough," he said. "But if you can cook, scars don't matter much."

Her mouth was open, and Leopold stomped on his big brother's foot, hard.

Callaghan popped him one on the arm with a fist the size of a ham. "Cut it out!"

"Don't insult her, she won't come!"

"I didn't!"

Reynard moved forward, elbowing the other two out of the way. He had his own hat in his hand. He tried to smile. It looked as if he hadn't had much practice at it.

"We'd like you to come tomorrow. Will you?"

She hesitated.

"Now see what you've done!" Leopold shot at Callaghan. "She's scared of us!"

"We wouldn't hurt you," Reynard said gently. He gave up trying to smile; it was unnatural anyway. "We have old Mrs. Culbertson keeping house for us. She carries a broomstick around with her. You'll be safe."

She bit back a laugh. But her eyes began to twinkle.

"She carries the broomstick because of him," Reynard added, indicating Leopold. "He likes to…"

"Never mind!" Leopold said icily.

"I was only going to say that you…"

"Shut up!"

"If you two don't stop, I'm going to lay you both out right here," Callaghan said, and looked very much as if he meant it. "Apologize."

They both murmured reluctant apologies.

"All right, that's that." He put his hat back on. "If you can come at nine, we'll send one of the boys for you."

"Thank you, I'd rather drive my own car."

"I've seen your car. That's why I'm sending one of the boys for you," Callaghan continued doggedly.

Her mouth fell open again. "It's a…a nice old car! And it runs fine!"

"Everybody knows Turkey Sanders sold it to you," Callaghan said with a disgusted look. "He's a pirate. You'll be lucky if the wheels don't fall off the first time you go around a curve."

"That's right," Rey agreed.

"We'll stop by on our way out of town and talk to him," Leopold said. "He'll bring your car back in and make sure it's perfectly safe to drive. He'll do it first thing tomorrow."

"But…"

They put their hats back on, gave her polite nods and stomped back out the way they'd come.

Callaghan paused at the front door, with the screen open. "He may talk and act tough, but he's hurt pretty bad, inside where it doesn't show. Don't hurt him again."

"Him?"

"Corrigan."

She moved forward, just a step. "It wasn't like that," she said gently. "He didn't feel anything for me."

"And you didn't, for him?"

She averted her gaze to the floor. "It was a long time ago."

"You shouldn't have left."

She looked back up, her eyes wide and wounded. "I was afraid of him!"

He let out a long breath. "You were just a kid. We tried to tell him. Even though we hadn't seen you, we knew about you from other people. We were pretty sure you weren't the sort of girl to play around. He wouldn't listen." He shrugged. "Maybe we corrupted him. You might ask him sometimes about our parents," he added coldly. "Kids don't grow up hating marriage without reason."

There was a lot of pain in his lean face. He was telling her things she'd never have dared ask Corrigan. She moved forward another step, aware of the other two talking out on the porch in hushed whispers.

"Is he still...like that?"

His eyes were cold, but as they looked into hers, they seemed to soften just a little. "He's not the same man he was. You'll have to find out the rest for yourself. We don't interfere in each other's lives, as a rule." His gaze went over her wan face. "You've been to hell and back, too."

He was as perceptive as his brother. She smiled. "I suppose it's part of becoming an adult. Losing illusions and dreams and hope, I mean." She locked her fingers together and looked up at him quietly. "Growing up is painful."

"Don't let go," he said suddenly. "No matter what he says, what he does, don't let go."

Her surprise widened her eyes. "Why?"

He pulled his hat lower over his forehead. "They don't make women like you anymore."

"Like me?" She frowned.

His dark eyes glittered. He smiled in a way that, if she hadn't been half-crazy about Corrigan, would have curled her toes. "I wish we'd met you before," he said. "You'd never have gotten on that bus." He tilted the hat. "We'll send Joey for you in the morning."

"But…"

The door closed behind him. He motioned to the other two and they followed him down the steps to the four-door pickup truck. It had a big cab. It was streamlined and black, and it had a menacing look not—unlike Corrigan Hart's brothers!

She wondered why they'd all come together to ask her to go out to the ranch, and why they'd done it when Corrigan was gone. She supposed she'd find out. She did wonder again about the fifth brother, the mysterious one that Corrigan had mentioned. None of these men were named Simon.

Later, the telephone rang, and it was Turkey Sanders. "I just wanted you to know that I'm going to have that car I sold you picked up in the morning and put to rights," he said at once. "I guarantee, it's going to be the best used car you've ever driven! If you would, just leave the keys in it, and I'll have it picked up first thing. And if there's anything else I can do for you, little lady, you just ask!"

He sounded much more enthusiastic than he had when he'd sold her the rusty little car. "Why, thank you," she said.

"No problem. None at all. Have a nice day, now."

He hung up and she stared blankly at the receiver. Well, nobody could say that living in Jacobsville wasn't interesting, she told herself. Apparently the brothers had a way with other businessmen, too. She'd never have admitted that the car had worried her from the time Turkey had talked her into buying it, for what seemed like a high price for such a wreck. She had a driver's license, which she had to have renewed. But never having owned a car in New York, it was unique to have one of her own, even if it did look like ten miles of bad road.

It was a cold, blustery morning when a polite young man drove up in a black Mercedes and held the door open for her.

"I'm Joey," he told her. "The brothers sent me to fetch you. I sure am glad you took on this job," he added. "They won't give me any money for gas until that checkbook's balanced. I've been having to syphon it out of their trucks with a hose." He shook his head ruefully as he waited for her to move her long denim skirt completely out of the door frame so that he could close the door. "I hate the taste of gasoline."

He closed the door, got in under the wheel and took off in a cloud of dust.

She smiled to herself. The brothers were strange people.

The ranch was immaculate, from its white wood fences to the ranch house itself, a long elegant brick home with a sprawling manicured lawn and a swimming pool and tennis court. The bunkhouse was brick, too, and the barn was so big that she imagined it could hold an entire herd of horses.

"Big, huh?" Joey grinned at her. "The brothers do things on a big scale, but they're meticulous—especially Cag. He runs the place, mostly."

"Cag?"

"Callaghan. Nobody calls him that in the family."

He glanced in her direction, amused. "They said you're the reason Corrigan never married."

Her heart jumped. "No kidding?"

"Oh, yeah. He doesn't even look at women these days. But when he heard that you were coming back, he shaved and bought new clothes." He shook his head. "Shocked us all, seeing him without a beard."

"I can't imagine him with one," she said with some confusion.

"Pity about his leg, but he's elegant on a horse, just the same."

"I think he gets around very well."

"Better than he used to." He pulled up in front of the house, turned off the engine and went around to help her out.

"It's right in here."

He led her in through the front door and down a carpeted hall to a pine-paneled office. "Mrs. Culbertson will be along any minute to get you some coffee or tea or a soft drink. The brothers had to get to work or they'd have been here to meet you. No worry, though, Corrigan's home. He'll be here shortly and show you the books. He's trying to doctor a colt, down in the barn."

"Thank you, Joey."

He tipped his hat. "My pleasure, ma'am." He gave her a cursory appraisal, nodded and went back out again.

He'd no sooner gone than a short, plump little woman with twinkling blue eyes and gray hair came in, rubbing her hands dry on her apron. "You'd be Miss Wayne. I'm Betty Culbertson," she introduced herself. "Can I get you a cup of coffee?"

"Oh, yes, please."

"Cream, sugar?"

"I like it black," she said.

The older woman grinned. "So do the boys. They don't like sweets, either. Hard to get fat around here, except on gravy and biscuits. They'd have those every meal if I'd cook them."

The questions the brothers had asked about her cooking came back to haunt her.

"None of them believe in marriage, do they?" she asked.

Mrs. Culbertson shook her head. "They've been bachelors too long now. They're set in their ways and none of them have much to do with women. Not that they aren't targeted by local belles," she added with a chuckle. "But nobody has much luck. Corrigan, now, he's mellowed. I hear it's because of you."

While Dorie flushed and tried to find the right words to answer her, a deep voice did it for her.

"Yes, it is," Corrigan said from the doorway. "But she isn't supposed to know it."

"Oops," Mrs. Culbertson said with a wicked chuckle. "Sorry."

He shrugged. "No harm done. I'll have coffee. So will she. And if you see Leopold…"

"I'll smash his skull for him, if I do," the elderly woman said abruptly, and her whole demeanor changed. Her blue eyes let off sparks. "That devil!"

"He did it again, I guess?"

She made an angry noise through her nose. "I've told him and told him…"

"You'd think he'd get tired of having that broom-

stick thrown at him, wouldn't you?'' Corrigan asked
pleasantly.

"One of these days he won't be quick enough,"
Mrs. Culbertson said with an evil smile.

"I'll talk to him."

"Everybody's already talked to him. It does no
good."

"What does he do?" Dorie asked curiously.

Mrs. Culbertson looked at Corrigan, who'd started
to answer, with eyes that promised culinary retribution.

"Sorry," he said abruptly. "I can't say."

Mrs. Culbertson nodded curtly and smiled at Dorie.
"I'll just get that coffee. Be back in a jiffy."

She left and Corrigan's dark eyes slid over Dorie's
pretty figure.

"You look very nice," he said. His eyes lifted to
her wavy hair and he smiled appreciatively. "I always
loved your hair. That was a first for me. Usually I
like a woman's hair long. Yours suits you just as it
is."

Her slender hand went to the platinum waves
self-consciously. "It's easy to keep like this." She
shifted to the other foot. "Your brothers came to the
house yesterday and asked me to come out here and
look at the household accounts. They say they're
starving."

"They look like it, too, don't they?" he asked disgustedly. "Good God, starving!"

"They were very nice," she continued. "They
talked to Turkey Sanders and he's repairing my car."

"His *mechanic's* repairing your car," he told her.
"Turkey's having a tooth fixed."

She knew she shouldn't ask. But she had to. "Why?"

"He made a remark that Cag didn't like."

"Cag. Oh, yes, he's the eldest."

He brightened when he realized that she remembered that. "He's thirty-eight, if you call that old." Anticipating her next question, he added blithely, "Leo's thirty-four. I'm thirty-six. Rey's thirty-two."

"So Cag hit Turkey Sanders?"

He shook his head.

"Then who broke his tooth?"

"Leo."

"Cag got mad, but Leo hit Turkey Sanders?" she asked, fascinated.

He nodded. "He did that to save him from Cag."

"I don't understand."

"Cag was in the Special Forces," he explained. "He was a captain when they sent him to the Middle East some years back." He shrugged. "He knows too much about hand-to-hand combat to be let loose in a temper. So we try to shield people from him." He grinned. "Leo figured that if he hit Turkey first, Cag wouldn't. And he didn't."

She just shook her head. "Your brothers are... unique," she said finally, having failed to find a good word to describe them.

He chuckled. "You don't know the half of it."

"Do they really hate women?"

"Sometimes," he said.

"I'll bet they're sought after," she mentioned, "especially when people get a good look at this ranch."

"The ranch is only a part of the properties we own," he replied. "Our people are fourth-generation

Texans, and we inherited thousands of acres of land and five ranches. They were almost bankrupt when the old man died, though," he mused. "He didn't really have a head for figures. Broke Grandad's heart. He saw the end of his empire. But we pulled it out of the fire."

"So I see," she agreed.

"The only problem is, none of us are married. So if we don't have descendants, who's going to keep the empire going?"

She thought of the most terrible answer to that question, and then got the giggles.

He raised an eyebrow.

She put a hand over her mouth until she got herself back under control. "Sorry. I was only thinking of that movie about the man who got pregnant...!"

He gave her a level look, unsmiling.

She cleared her throat. "Where are the accounts?"

He hesitated for a minute, and then opened the desk drawer and took out a set of ledgers, placing them on the spotless cherry wood desk.

"This is beautiful," she remarked, stroking the silky, high-polished surface.

"It was our grandfather's," he told her. "We didn't want to change things around too much. The old gentleman was fond of the office just the way it is."

She looked around, puzzled by the plain wood paneling. There were no deer heads or weapons anywhere. She said so.

"He didn't like trophies," he told her. "Neither do we. If we hunt, we use every part of the deer, but we don't have the heads mounted. It doesn't seem quite sporting.''

She turned as she pulled out the desk chair, and looked at him with open curiosity.

"None of your brothers are like I pictured them."

"In what way?"

She smiled. "You're very handsome," she said, averting her eyes when his began to glitter. "They aren't. And they all have very dark eyes. Yours are gray, like mine."

"They favor our mother," he said. "I favor him." He nodded toward the one portrait, on the wall behind the desk. It looked early twentieth century and featured a man very like Corrigan, except with silver hair.

"So that's what you'll look like," she remarked absently.

"Eventually. Not for a few years, I hope."

She glanced at him, because he'd come to stand beside her. "You're going gray, just at the temples."

He looked down into her soft face. His eyes narrowed as he searched every inch of her above the neck. "Gray won't show in that beautiful mop on your head," he said quietly. "It'll blend in and make it even prettier."

The comment was softly spoken, and so poetic that it embarrassed her. She smiled self-consciously and her gaze fell to his shirt. It was open at the collar, because it was warm in the house. Thick black hair peered over the button, and unwanted memories of that last night they'd been together came flooding back. He'd taken his shirt off, to give her hands total access to his broad, hair-roughened chest. He liked her lips on it...

She cleared her throat and looked away, her color high. "I'd better get to work."

His lean hand caught her arm, very gently, and he pulled her back around. His free hand went to the snaps that held the shirt together. He looked into her startled eyes and slowly, one by one, he flicked the snaps apart.

"What...are you...doing?" she faltered. She couldn't breathe. He was weaving spells around her. She felt weak-kneed already, and the sight of that broad chest completely bare drew a faint gasp from her lips.

He had her by the elbows. He drew her to him, so that her lips were on a level with his collarbone. She could hear his heartbeat, actually hear it.

"It was like this," he said in a raw, ragged tone. "But I had your blouse off, your breasts bare. I drew you to me, like this," he whispered unsteadily, drawing her against the length of him, "and I bent, and took your open mouth under my own...like this..."

It was happening all over again. She was eight years older, but apparently not one day less vulnerable. He put her cold hands into the thick hair on his chest and moved them while his hard mouth took slow, sweet possession of her lips.

He nudged her lips apart and hesitated for just a second, long enough to look into her eyes and see the submission and faint hunger in them. There was just the hint of a smile on his lips before he parted them against her soft mouth.

Chapter 4

She had no pride at all, she decided in the hectic seconds that followed the first touch of his hard mouth. She was a total washout as a liberated woman.

His hands had gone to her waist and then moved up to her rib cage, to the soft underside of her breasts. He stroked just under them until she shivered and moaned, and then his hands lifted and took possession; blatant possession.

He felt her mouth open. His own answered it while he touched her, searched over her breasts and found the hard nipples that pushed against his palms.

His mouth grew rougher. She felt his hands move around her, felt the catch give. Her blouse was pushed up with a shivering urgency, and seconds later, her bare breasts were buried in the thick hair that covered his chest and abdomen.

She cried out, dragging her mouth from his.

He looked into her eyes, but he wouldn't let her go. His hard face was expressionless. Only his eyes were alive, glittering like gray fires. He deliberately moved her from side to side and watched her face as he did it, enjoying, with a completely masculine delight, the pleasure she couldn't hide.

"Your nipples are like rocks against me." He bit off the words, holding her even closer. "I took your breasts inside my mouth the night we made love, and you arched up right off the bed to give them to me. Do you remember what you did next?"

She couldn't speak. She looked at him with mingled desire and fear.

"You slid your hands inside my jeans," he whispered roughly. "And you touched me. That's when I lost control."

Her moan was one of shame, not pleasure. She found his chest with her cheek and pressed close to him, shivering. "I'm sorry," she whispered brokenly. "I'm so sorry...!"

His mouth found her eyes and kissed them shut. "Don't," he whispered roughly. "I'm not saying it to shame you. I only want you to remember why it ended the way it did. You were grass green and I didn't know it. I encouraged you to be uninhibited, but I'd never have done it if I'd known what an innocent you were." His mouth slid over her forehead with breathless tenderness while his hands slid to her lower back and pulled her even closer. "I was going to take you," he whispered. His hands contracted and his body went rigid with a surge of arousal that she could feel. His legs trembled. "I still want to, God help me," he breathed at her temple. "I've never had

the sort of arousal I feel with you. I don't even have
to undress you first.'' His hands began to tremble as
he moved her sensually against his hips. His mouth
slid down to hers and softly covered it, lifting and
touching and probing until she shivered again with
pleasure.

"I thought you knew," she whimpered.

"I didn't.'' His hands moved to the very base of
her spine and lifted her gently into the hard thrust of
his body. He caught his breath at the wave of pleasure
that washed over him immediately. "Dorie," he
breathed.

She couldn't think at all. When he took one of her
hands and pressed it to his lower body, she didn't
even have the will to protest. Her hand opened and
she let him move it gently against him, on fire with
the need to touch him.

"Eight years," she said shakily.

"And we're still starving for each other," he whispered at her mouth. His hand became insistent.
"Harder," he said and his breath caught.

"This…isn't wise," she said against his chest.

"No, but it's sweet. Dorie…!" He cried out
hoarsely, his whole body shuddering.

Her hand stilled at once. "I'm sorry," she whispered frantically. "Did I hurt you?"

He wasn't breathing normally at all. His face was
buried in her throat and he was shaking like a leaf.
She brushed her mouth over his cheek, his chin, his
lips, his nose, whispering his name as she clung to
him.

His hand gripped her upper thigh, and it was so
bruising that she was afraid she was going to have to

protest. He fought for sanity, embarrassed by his weakness.

She was still kissing him. He felt her breasts moving against his chest, intensifying the throbbing, hellish ache below his belt.

He held her firmly in place with hands that shook. She subsided and stood quietly against him. She knew now, as she hadn't eight years ago, what was wrong with him. She felt guilty and ashamed for pushing him so far out of control.

Her fingers touched his thick, cool hair lovingly. Her lips found his eyelids and brushed softly against them. He was vulnerable and she wanted to protect him, cherish him.

The tenderness was doing strange things to him. He still wanted her to the point of madness, but those comforting little kisses made his heart warm. He'd never been touched in such a way by a woman; he'd never felt so cherished.

She drew back, and he pulled her close again.

"Don't stop," he whispered, calmer now. His hands had moved up to the silken skin of her back, and he smiled under the whisper of her lips on his skin.

"I'm so sorry," she whispered.

His fingers slid under the blouse again and up to explore the softness of her breasts. "Why?" he asked.

"You were hurting," she said. "I shouldn't have touched you..."

He chuckled wickedly. "I made you."

"I still can't go to bed with you," she said miserably. "I don't care if the whole world does it, I just can't!"

His hands opened and enfolded her breasts tenderly. "You want to," he murmured as he caressed them.

"Of course I want to!" Her eyes closed and she swayed closer to his hands. "Oh, glory," she managed to say tightly, shivering.

"Your breasts are very sensitive," he said at her lips. "And soft like warm silk under my hands. I'd like to lay you down on my grandfather's desk and take your blouse off and put my lips on you there. But Mrs. Culbertson is making coffee." He lifted his head and looked into her dazed, soft gray eyes. "Thank God," he whispered absently as he searched them.

"Thank God for what?" she asked huskily.

"Miracles, maybe," he replied. He smoothed the blouse up again and his eyes sketched her pretty pink breasts with their hard dark pink crowns. "I could eat you like taffy right now," he said in a rough tone.

The office was so quiet that not a sound could be heard above the shiver of her breath as she looked up at him.

His pale eyes were almost apologetic. "I think I have a death wish," he began huskily as he bent.

She watched his mouth hover over her breast with a sense of shocked wonder. Her eyes wide, her breath stopped in her throat, she waited, trembling.

He looked up, then, and saw her eyes. He made a sound in the back of his throat and his mouth opened as he propelled her closer, so that he had her almost completely in that warm, moist recess.

She wept. The pleasure grew to unbearable heights. Her fingers tangled in his hair and she pulled him closer. She growled sharply at the sensations she felt. Her hips moved involuntarily, searching for his body.

The suction became so sweet that she suddenly arched backward, and would have fallen if it hadn't been for his supporting arm. She caught her breath and convulsed, her body frozen in an arc of pure ecstasy.

He felt the deep contractions of her body under his mouth with raging pride. His mouth grew a little rough, and the convulsions deepened.

Only when he felt her begin to relax did he lift his head and bring her back into a standing position, so that he could look at her face.

She couldn't breathe. She sobbed as she looked up into his pale eyes. The tears came, hot and quick, when she realized what had happened. And he'd seen it!

"Don't," he chided tenderly. He reached for a handkerchief and dried her red eyes and wiped her nose. "Don't be embarrassed."

"I could die of shame," she wept.

"For what?" he asked softly. "For letting me watch you?"

Her face went red. "I never, never…!"

He put a long forefinger against her lips. "I've never seen a woman like that," he whispered. "I've never known one who could be satisfied by a man's mouth suckling at her breast. It was the most beautiful experience I've ever had."

She wasn't crying now. She was staring at him, her eyes wide and soft and curious.

He brushed back her wild hair. "It was worth what I felt earlier," he murmured dryly.

She colored even more. "I can't stay here," she told him wildly. "I have to go away…"

"Hell, no, you don't," he said tersely. "You're not getting away from me a second time. Don't even think about running."

"But," she began urgently.

"But what?" he asked curtly. "But you can't give yourself to me outside marriage? I know that. I'm not asking you to sleep with me."

"It's like torture for you."

"Yes," he said simply. "But the alternative is to never touch you." His hand slid over her blouse and he smiled gently at the immediate response of her body. "I love this," he said gruffly. "And so do you."

She grimaced. "Of course I do," she muttered. "I've never let anyone else touch me like that. It's been eight years since I've even been kissed!"

"Same here," he said bluntly.

"Ha! You've been going around with a divorcée!" she flung at him out of frustration and embarrassment.

"I don't have sex with her," he said.

"They say she's very pretty."

He smiled. "She is. Pretty and elegant and kind. But I don't feel desire for her, any more than she feels it for me. I told you we were friends. We are. And that's all we are."

"But…but…"

"But what, Dorie?"

"Men don't stop kissing women just because they get turned down once."

"It was much worse than just getting turned down," he told her. "I ran you out of town. It was rough living with that, especially when your father took a few strips off me and told me all about your past. I felt two inches high.'' His eyes darkened with the pain of the memory. ''I hated having made an enemy of him. He was a good man. But I'd never had much interest in marriage or let anyone get as close to me as you did. If you were afraid, so was I.''

''Cag said your parents weren't a happy couple.''

His eyebrow lifted. ''He never talks about them. That's a first.''

''He told me to ask you about them.''

''I see.'' He sighed. ''Well, I told you a little about that, but we're going to have to talk more about them sooner or later, and about some other things.'' He lifted his head and listened and then looked down at her with a wicked grin. ''But for the present, you'd better fasten your bra and tuck your blouse back in and try to look as if you haven't just made love with me.''

''Why?''

''Mrs. Culbertson's coming down the hall.''

''Oh, my gosh!''

She fumbled with catches and buttons, her face red, her hair wild as she raced to put herself back together. He snapped his shirt up lazily, his silvery eyes full of mischief as he watched her frantic efforts to improve her appearance.

''Lucky I didn't lay you down on the desk, isn't it?'' he said, chuckling.

There was a tap on the half-closed door and Mrs. Culbertson came in with a tray. She was so intent on getting it to the desk intact that she didn't even look at Dorie.

"Here it is. Sorry I took so long, but I couldn't find the cream pitcher."

"Who drinks cream?" Corrigan asked curiously.

"It was the only excuse I could think of," she told him seriously.

He looked uneasy. "Thanks."

She grinned at him and then looked at Dorie. Her eyes were twinkling as she went back out. And this time she closed the door.

Dorie's face was still flushed. Her gray eyes were wide and turbulent. Her mouth was swollen and when she folded her arms over her chest, she flinched.

His eyes went to her blouse and back up again. "When I felt you going over the edge, it excited me, and I got a little rough. Did I hurt you?"

The question was matter-of-fact, and strangely tender.

She shook her head, averting her eyes. It was embarrassing to remember what had happened.

He caught her hand and led her to the chairs in front of the desk. "Sit down and I'll pour you a cup of coffee."

She looked up at him a little uneasily. "Is something wrong with me, do you think?" she asked with honest concern. "I mean, it's unnatural...isn't it?"

His fingers touched her soft cheek. He shook his head. "People can't be pigeonholed. You might not be that responsive to any other man. Maybe it's waiting so long. Maybe it's that you're perfectly attuned to me. I might be able to accomplish the same thing by kissing your thighs, or your belly."

She flushed. "You wouldn't!"

"Why not?"

The thought of it made her vibrate all over. She knew that men kissed women in intimate places, but she hadn't quite connected it until then.

"The inside of your thighs is very vulnerable to being caressed," he said simply. "Not to mention your back, your hips, your feet," he added with a gentle smile. "Lovemaking is an art. There are no set rules."

She watched him turn and pour coffee into a ceramic cup. He handed it to her and watched the way her fingers deliberately touched his as she drew them away.

He wanted her so much that he could barely stand up straight, but it was early days yet. He had to go slowly this time and not push her too hard. She had a fear not only of him, but of real intimacy. He couldn't afford to let things go too far.

"What sort of things are we going to talk about later?" she asked after she'd finished half her coffee.

"Cabbages and kings," he mused. He sat across from her, his long legs crossed, his eyes possessive and caressing on her face.

"I don't like cabbage and I don't know any kings."

"Then suppose we lie down together on the sofa?"

Her eyes flashed up to see the amusement in his and back down to her cup. "Don't tease. I'm not sophisticated enough for it."

"I'm not teasing."

She sighed and took another sip of coffee. "There's no future in it. You know that."

He didn't know it. She was living in the past, convinced that he had nothing more than an affair in mind for them. He smiled secretively to himself as he thought about the future. Fate had given him a second chance; he wasn't going to waste it.

"About these books," he said in a businesslike tone. "I've made an effort with them, but although I can do math, my penmanship isn't what it should be. If you can't read any of the numbers, circle them and I'll tell you what they are. I have to meet a prospective buyer down at the barn in a few minutes, but I'll be somewhere close by all day."

"All right."

He finished his coffee and put the cup back on the tray, checking his watch. "I'd better go." He looked down at her with covetous eyes and leaned against the arms of her chair to study her. "Let's go dancing tomorrow night."

Her heart jumped. She was remembering how it was when they were close together and her face flushed.

His eyebrow lifted and he grinned. "Don't look so apprehensive. The time to worry is when nothing happens when I hold you."

"It always did," she replied.

He nodded. "Every time," he agreed. "I only had to touch you." He smiled softly. "And vice versa," he added with a wicked glance.

"I was green," she reminded him.

"You still are," he reminded her.

"Not so much," she ventured shyly.

"We both learned something today," he said quietly. "Dorie, if you can be satisfied by so small a caress, try to imagine how it would feel if we went all the way."

Her eyelids flickered. Her breath came like rustling leaves.

He bent and drew his mouth with exquisite tenderness over her parted lips. "Or is that the real problem?" he asked at her mouth. "Are you afraid of the actual penetration?"

Her heart stopped dead and then ran away. "Corrigan!" She ground out his name.

He drew back a breath so that he could see her eyes. He wasn't smiling. It was no joke.

"You'd better tell me," he said quietly.

She drew her lower lip in with her teeth, looking worried.

"I won't tell anyone."

"I know that." She took a long breath. "When my cousin Mary was married, she came to visit us after the honeymoon was over. She'd been so happy and excited." She grimaced. "She said that it hurt awfully bad, that she bled and bled, and he made fun of her because she cried. She said that he didn't even kiss her. He just…pushed into her…!"

He cursed under his breath. "Didn't you talk to anyone else about sex?"

"It wasn't something I could discuss with my father, and Mary was the only friend I had," she told him. "She said that all the things they write about are just fiction, and that the reality is just like her mother once said—a woman deals with it for the pleasure of children."

He leaned forward on his hands, shaking his head. "I wish you'd told me this eight years ago."

"You'd have laughed," she replied. "You didn't believe I was innocent anyway."

He looked up into her eyes. "I'm sorry," he said heavily. "Life teaches hard lessons."

She thought about her own experience with modeling. "Yes, it does."

He got to his feet and looked down at her with a worried scowl. "Don't you watch hot movies?"

"Those women aren't virgins," she returned.

"No. I don't guess they are." His eyes narrowed as he searched her face. "And I don't know what to tell you. I've never touched an innocent woman until you came along. Maybe it does hurt. But I promise you, it would only be one time. I know enough to make it good for you. And I would."

"It isn't going to be that way," she reminded him tersely, denying herself the dreams of marriage and children that she'd always connected with him. "We're going to be friends."

He didn't speak. His gaze didn't falter. "I'll check back with you later about the books," he said quietly.

"Okay."

He started to turn, thought better of it and leaned down again with his weight balanced on the chair arms. "Do you remember what happened when I started to suckle you?"

She went scarlet. "Please..."

"It will be like that," he said evenly. "Just like that. You won't think about pain. You may not even notice any. You go in headfirst when I touch you. And I wasn't even taking my time with you today. Think about that. It might help."

He pushed away from her again and went to the desk to pick up his hat. He placed it on his head and smiled at her without mockery.

"Don't let my brothers walk over you," he said. "If one of them gives you any trouble, lay into him with the first hard object you can get your hands on."

"They seem very nice," she said.

"They like you," he replied. "But they have plans."

"Plans?"

"Not to hurt you," he assured her. "You should never have told them you could cook."

"I don't understand."

"Mrs. Culbertson wants to quit. They can't make biscuits. It's what they live for, a plateful of home-made buttered biscuits with half a dozen jars of jam and jelly."

"How does that concern me?"

"Don't you know?" He perched himself against the desk. "They've decided that we should marry you."

"*We?*"

"We're a family. Mostly we share things. Not women, but we do share cooks." He cocked his head and grinned at her shocked face. "If I marry you, they don't have to worry about where their next fresh biscuit is coming from."

"You don't want to marry me."

"Well, they'll probably find some way around that," he said pointedly.

"They can't force you to marry me."

"I wouldn't make any bets on that," he said. "You don't know them yet."

"You're their brother. They'd want you to be happy."

"They think you'll make me happy."

She lowered her eyes. "You should talk to them."

"And say what? That I don't want you? I don't think they'd believe me."

"I meant, you should tell them that you don't want to get married."

"They've already had a meeting and decided that I do. They've picked out a minister and a dress that they think you'll look lovely in. They've done a rough draft of a wedding invitation..."

"You're out of your mind!"

"No, I'm not." He went to the middle desk drawer, fumbled through it, pulled it further out and reached for something pushed to the very back of the desk. He produced it, scanned it, nodded and handed it to her. "Read that."

It was a wedding invitation. Her middle name was misspelled. "It's Ellen, not Ellis."

He reached behind him for a pen, took the invitation back, made the change and handed it back to her.

"Why did you do that?" she asked curiously.

"Oh, they like everything neat and correct."

"Don't correct it! Tear it up!"

"They'll just do another one. The papers will print what's on there, too. You don't want your middle name misspelled several thousand times, do you?"

She was all but gasping for breath. "I don't understand."

"I know. Don't worry about it right now. There's plenty of time. They haven't decided on a definite date yet, anyway."

She stood up, wild-eyed. "You can't let your

brothers decide when and who you're going to marry!''

''Well, you go stop them, then,'' he said easily. ''But don't say I didn't tell you so.''

He pulled his hat over his eyes and walked out the door, whistling softly to himself.

Chapter 5

First she did the accounts. Her mind was still reeling from Corrigan's ardor, and she had to be collected when she spoke to his brothers. She deciphered his scribbled numbers, balanced the books, checked her figures and put down a total.

They certainly weren't broke, and there was enough money in the account to feed Patton's Third Army. She left them a note saying so, amused at the pathetic picture they'd painted of their finances. Probably, the reason for that was part of their master plan.

She went outside to look for them after she'd done the books. They were all four in the barn, standing close together. They stopped talking the minute she came into view, and she knew for certain that they'd been talking about her.

"I'm not marrying him," she told them clearly, and pointed at Corrigan.

"Okay," Leo said easily.

"The thought never crossed my mind," Rey remarked.

Cag just shrugged.

Corrigan grinned.

"I'm through with the books," she said uneasily. "I want to go home now."

"You haven't eaten lunch," Rey said.

"It's only eleven o'clock," she said pointedly.

"We have an early lunch, because we work until dark," Cag volunteered.

"Mrs. Culbertson just left," Rey said. He sighed. "She put some beef and gravy in the oven to warm. But she didn't make us any biscuits."

"We don't have anything to put gravy on," Leo agreed.

"Can't work all afternoon without a biscuit," Cag said, nodding.

Corrigan grinned.

Dorie had thought that Corrigan was making up that story about the brothers' mania for biscuits. Apparently it was the gospel truth.

"Just one pan full," Leo coaxed. "It wouldn't take five minutes." He eyed her warily. "If you can really make them. Maybe you can't. Maybe you were just saying you could, to impress us."

"That's right," Rey added.

"I can make biscuits," she said, needled. "You just point me to the kitchen and I'll show you."

Leo grinned. "Right this way!"

Half an hour later, the pan of biscuits were gone so fast that they might have disintegrated. Leo and

Corrigan were actually fighting over the last one, pulled it apart in their rush, and ended up splitting it while the other two sat there gloating. They'd had more than their share because they had faster hands.

"Next time, you've got to make two pans," Corrigan told her. "One doesn't fill Leo's hollow tooth."

"I noticed," she said, surprisingly touched by the way they'd eaten her biscuits with such enjoyment. "I'll make you a pan of rolls to go with them next time."

"Rolls?" Leo looked faint. *"You can make home-made rolls?"*

"I'll see about the wedding rings right now," Rey said, wiping his mouth and pushing away from the table.

"I've got the corrected invitation in my pocket," Cag murmured as he got up, too.

Leo joined the other two at the door. "They said they can get the dress here from Paris in two weeks," Leo said.

Dorie gaped at them. But before she could open her mouth, all three of them had rushed out the door and closed it, talking animatedly among themselves.

"But, I didn't say...!" she exclaimed.

"There, there," Corrigan said, deftly adding another spoonful of gravy to his own remaining half of a biscuit. "It's all right. They forgot to call the minister and book him."

Just at that moment, the door opened and Leo stuck his head in. "Are you Methodist, Baptist or Presbyterian?" he asked her.

"I'm...Presbyterian," she faltered.

He scowled. "Nearest Presbyterian minister is in

Victoria,'' he murmured thoughtfully, "but don't worry, I'll get him here." He closed the door.

"Just a minute!" she called.

The doors of the pickup closed three times. The engine roared. "Too late," Corrigan said imperturbably.

"But didn't you hear him?" she burst out. "For heaven's sake, they're going to get a minister!"

"Hard to get married in church without one," he insisted. He gestured toward her plate with a fork to the remaining chunk of beef. "Don't waste that. It's one of our own steers. Corn fed, no hormones, no antibiotics, no insecticides. We run a clean, environmentally safe operation here."

She was diverted. "Really?"

"We're renegades," he told her. "They groan when they see us coming at cattle conventions. Usually we go with Donavan. He's just like us about cattle. He and the Ballenger brothers have gone several rounds over cattle prods and feed additives. He's mellowed a bit since his nephew came to live with him and he got married. But he likes the way we do things."

"I guess so." She savored the last of the beef. "It's really good."

"Beats eating pigs," he remarked, and grinned.

She burst out laughing. "Your brother Cag had plenty to say on that subject."

"He only eats beef or fish. He won't touch anything that comes from a pig. He says it's because he doesn't like the taste." He leaned forward conspiratorially. "But I say it's because of that movie he went to see. He used to love a nice ham."

"What movie?"

"The one with the talking pig."

"Cag went to see *that?*"

"He likes cartoons and sentimental movies." He shrugged. "Odd, isn't it? He's the most staid of us. To look at him, you'd never know he had a sense of humor or that he was sentimental. He's like the others in his lack of conventional good looks, though. Most women can't get past that big nose and those eyes."

"A cobra with a rabbit," she said without thinking.

He chuckled. "Exactly."

"Does he hate women as much as the rest of you?"

"Hard to tell. You haven't seen him in a tuxedo at a social bash. Women, really beautiful women, followed him around all night dropping their room keys at his feet."

"What did he do?"

"Kept walking."

She put down her fork. "What do you do?"

He smiled mockingly. "They don't drop room keys at my feet anymore. The limp puts them off."

"Baloney," she said. "You're the handsomest of the four, and it isn't just looks."

He leaned back in his chair to look at her. His eyes narrowed thoughtfully. "Does the limp bother you?"

"Don't be ridiculous," she said, lifting her gaze. "Why should it?"

"I can't dance very well anymore."

She smiled. "I don't ever go to dances."

"Why not?"

She sipped coffee. "I don't like men touching me."

His eyes changed. "You like me touching you."

"You aren't a stranger," she said simply.

"Maybe I am," he murmured quietly. "What do you know about me?"

She stared at him. "Well, you're thirty-six, you're a rancher, you've never married, you come from San Antonio."

"And?"

"I don't know any more than that," she said slowly.

"We were a couple for several weeks before you left town. Is that all you learned?"

"You were always such a private person," she reminded him. "You never talked about yourself or your brothers. And we never really talked that much when we were together."

"We spent more time kissing," he recalled. "I was too wrapped up in trying to get you into bed to care how well we knew each other," he said with self-contempt. "I wasted a lot of time."

"You said that we shouldn't look back."

"I'm trying not to. It's hard, sometimes." He moved forward to take her hands under his on the table. "I like classical music, but I'm just as happy with country or pop. I like a good chess game. I enjoy science fiction movies and old Westerns, the silent kind. I'm an early riser, I work hard and I don't cheat on my tax returns. I went to college to learn animal husbandry, but I never graduated."

She smiled. "Do you like fried liver?"

He made a horrible face. "Do you?"

She made the same face. "But I don't like sweets very much, either," she said, remembering that he didn't.

"Good thing. Nobody around here eats them."

"I remember." She looked around at the comfortably big kitchen. There was a new electric stove and a huge refrigerator, flanked by an upright freezer. The sink was a double stainless-steel one, with a window above it overlooking the pasture where the colts were kept. Next to that was a dishwasher. There was plenty of cabinet space, too.

"Like it?" he asked.

She smiled. "It's a dream of a kitchen. I'll bet Mrs. Culbertson loves working in here."

"Would you?"

She met his eyes and felt her own flickering at the intensity of his stare.

"If you can make homemade bread, you have to be an accomplished cook," he continued. "There's a high-tech mixer in the cabinet, and every gourmet tool known to man. Or woman."

"It's very modern."

"It's going to be very deserted in about three weeks," he informed.

"Why is Mrs. Culbertson quitting?"

"Her husband has cancer, and she wants to retire and stay at home with him, for as long as he's got," he said abruptly. He toyed with his coffee cup. "They've been married for fifty years." He took a sharp breath, and his eyes were very dark as they met hers. "I've believed all my life that no marriage could possibly last longer than a few years. People change. Situations change. Jobs conflict." He shrugged. "Then Mrs. Culbertson came here to work, with her husband. And I had to eat my words." He lowered his eyes back to the cup. "They were forever holding hands, helping each other, walking in the early morning together and talking. She smiled at him, and she was beautiful. He smiled back. Nobody had to say that they loved each other. It was obvious.''

"My parents were like that," she recalled. "Dad and Mom loved each other terribly. When she died, I almost lost him, too. He lived for me. But the last thing he said on his deathbed—" she swallowed, fighting tears "—was her name."

He got up from the table abruptly and went to the window over the sink. He leaned against it, breathing heavily, as if what she'd said had affected him powerfully. And, in fact, it had.

She watched him through tears. "You don't like hearing about happy marriages. Why?"

"Because I had that same chance once," he said in a low, dull tone. "And I threw it away."

She wondered who the woman had been. Nobody had said that any of the Hart brothers had ever been engaged. But there could have been someone she hadn't heard about.

"You're the one who keeps saying we can't look back," she remarked, dabbing her eyes with her napkin.

"It's impossible not to. The past makes us the people we are." He sighed wearily. "My parents had five of us in ten years. My mother hadn't wanted the first child. She didn't have a choice. He took away her checkbook and kept her pregnant. She hated him and us in equal measure. When she left it was almost a relief." He turned and looked across the room at her. "I've never been held with tenderness. None of us have. It's why we're the way we are, it's why we don't have women around. The only thing we know about women is that they're treacherous and cold and cruel."

"Oh, Corrigan," she said softly, wincing.

His eyes narrowed. "Desire is a hot and unmanageable thing. Sex can be pleasant enough. But I'd gladly be impotent to have a woman hold me the way you did in my office and kiss my eyes." His face went as hard as stone. "You can't imagine how it felt."

"But I can," she replied. She smiled. "You kissed my eyes."

"Yes."

He looked so lost, so lonely. She got up from the table and went to him, paused in front of him. Her hands pressed gently against his broad chest as she looked up into his eyes.

"You know more about me than I've ever told anyone else," he said quietly. "Now don't you think it's time you told me what happened to you in New York?"

She sighed worriedly. She'd been ashamed to tell him how stupid she'd been. But now there was a bigger reason. It was going to hurt him. She didn't understand how she knew it, but she did. He was going to blame himself all over again for the way they'd separated.

"Not now," she said.

"You're holding back. Don't let's have secrets between us," he said solemnly.

"It will hurt," she said.

"Most everything does, these days," he murmured, and rubbed his thigh.

She took his hand and held it warmly. "Come and sit down."

"Not in here."

He drew her into the living room. It was warm and dim and quiet. He led her to his big armchair, dropped into it and pulled her down into his arms.

"Now, tell me," he said, when her cheek was pillowed on his hard chest.

"It's not a nice story."

"Tell me."

She rubbed her hand against his shirt and closed her eyes. "I found an ad in the paper. It was one of those big ads that promise the stars, just the thing to appeal to a naive country girl who thinks she can just walk into a modeling career. I cut out the ad and called the number."

"And?"

She grimaced. "It was a scam, but I didn't know it at first. The man seemed very nice, and he had a studio in a good part of town. Belinda had gone to Europe for the week on an assignment for the magazine where she worked, and I didn't know anyone else to ask about it. I assumed that it was legitimate." Her eyes closed and she pressed closer, feeling his arm come around her tightly, as if he knew she was seeking comfort.

"Go ahead," he coaxed gently.

"He gave me a few things to try on and he took pictures of me wearing them. But then I was sitting there, just in a two-piece bathing suit, and he told me to take it off." His breathing stilled under her ear. "I couldn't," she snapped. "I just couldn't let him look at me like that, no matter how good a job I could get, and I said so. Then he got ugly. He told me that he was in the business of producing nude calendars and that if I didn't do the assignment, he'd take me to court and sue me for not fulfilling the contract I'd signed. No, I didn't read it," she said when he asked. "The fine print did say that I agreed to pose in any manner the photographer said for me to. I knew that I couldn't afford a lawsuit."

"And?" He sounded as cold as ice.

She bit her lower lip. "While I was thinking about alternatives, he laughed and came toward me. I could forget the contract, he said, if I was that prudish. But he'd have a return for the time he'd wasted on me. He said that he was going to make me sleep with him."

"Good God!"

She smoothed his shirt, trying to calm him. Tears stung her eyes. "I fought him, but I wasn't strong enough. He had me undressed before I knew it. We struggled there on the floor and he started hitting me." Her voice broke and she felt Corrigan stiffen against her. "He had a diamond ring on his right hand. That's how he cut my cheek. I didn't even feel it until much later. He wore me down to the point that I couldn't kick or bite or scream. I would never have been able to get away. But one of his girls, one of the ones who didn't mind posing nude, came into the studio. She was his lover and she was furious when she saw him with me...like that. She started screaming and throwing things at him. I grabbed my clothes and ran."

She shivered even then with the remembered humiliation, the fear that he was going to come after her. "I managed to get enough on to look halfway decent, and I walked all the way back to Belinda's apartment." She swallowed. "When I was rational enough to talk, I called the police. They arrested him and charged him with attempted rape. But he said that I'd signed a contract and I wasn't happy with the money he offered me, and that I'd only yelled rape because I wanted to back out of the deal."

He bit off a curse. "And then what?"

"He won," she said in a flat, defeated tone. "He had friends and influence. But the story was a big deal locally for two or three days, and he was furious. His brother had a nasty temper and he started making obscene phone calls to me and making threats as well. I didn't want to put Belinda in any danger, so I moved out while she was still in Europe and never told her a thing about what had happened. I got a job in New Jersey and worked there for two years. Then Belinda moved out to Long Island and asked me to come back. There was a good job going with a law firm that had an office pretty close to her house. I had good typing skills by then, so I took it."

"What about the brother?" he asked.

"He didn't know where to find me. I learned later that he and the photographer were having trouble with the police about some pornography ring they were involved in. Ironically they both went to prison soon after I left Manhattan. But for a long time, I was even afraid to come home, in case they had anyone watching me. I was afraid for my father."

"You poor kid," he said heavily. "Good God! And after what had happened here..." His teeth ground together as he remembered what he'd done to her.

"Don't," she said gently, smoothing out the frown between his heavy eyebrows. "I never blamed you. Never!"

He caught her hand and brought it to his mouth. "I wanted to come after you," he said. "Your father stopped me. He said that you hated the very mention of my name."

"I did, at first, but only because I was so hurt by the way things had worked out." She looked at his firm chin. "But I would have been glad to see you, just the same."

"I wasn't sure of that." He traced her mouth. "I thought that it might be as well to leave things the way they were. You were so young, and I was wary of complications in my life just then." He sighed softly. "There's one other thing you don't know about me."

"Can't you tell me?"

He smiled softly. "We're sharing our deepest secrets. I suppose I might as well. We have a fifth brother. His name is Simon."

"You mentioned him the first time you came over, with that bouquet."

He nodded. "He's in San Antonio. Just after you left town, he was in a wreck and afterward, in a coma. We couldn't all go back, and leave the ranch to itself. So I went. It was several weeks before I could leave him. By the time I got back, you weren't living with Belinda anymore and I couldn't make her tell me where you were. Soon after that, your father came down on my head like a brick and I lost heart."

"You called Belinda?"

"Yes."

"You wanted to find me?"

He searched her eyes quietly. "I wanted to know that you were safe, that I hadn't hurt you too badly. At least I found that much out. I didn't hope for more."

She traced his eyebrows, lost in the sudden intimacy. "I dreamed about you," she said. "But every time, you'd come toward me and I'd wake up."

He traced the artery in her throat down to her collarbone. "My dreams were a bit more erotic." His eyes darkened. "I had you in ways and places you can't imagine, each more heated than the one before. I couldn't wait to go to bed, so that I could have you again."

She blushed. "At first, you mean, just after I left."

His hand smoothed onto her throat. "For eight years. Every night of my life."

She caught her breath. She could hardly get it at all. His eyes were glittering with feeling. "All that time?"

He nodded. He looked at her soft throat where the blouse had parted, and his face hardened. His fingers trailed lightly down onto her bodice, onto her breast. "I haven't touched a woman since you left Jacobsville," he said huskily. "I haven't been a man since then."

Her wide eyes filled with tears. She had a good idea of what it would be like for a man like Corrigan to be incapable with a woman. "Was it because we fought, at the last?"

"It was because we made love," he whispered. "Have you forgotten what we did?"

She averted her eyes, hiding them in embarrassment.

"You left a virgin," he said quietly, "but only technically. We had each other in your bed," he reminded her, "naked in each other's arms. We did everything except go those last few aching inches. Your body was almost open to me, I was against you, we were moving together…and you cried out when you felt me there. You squirmed out from under me and ran."

"I was so afraid," she whispered shamefully. "It hurt, and I kept remembering what I'd been told…"

"It wouldn't have hurt for long," he said gently. "And it wouldn't have been traumatic, not for you. But you didn't know that, and I was too excited to coax you. I lost my temper instead of reassuring you. And we spent so many years apart, suffering for it."

She laid her hot cheek against his chest and closed her eyes. "I didn't want to remember how far we went," she said through a mist. "I hurt you terribly when I drew back…"

"Not that much," he said. "We'd made love in so many ways already that I wasn't that hungry." He smoothed her soft hair. "I wanted an excuse to make you leave."

"Why?"

His lips touched her hair. "Because I wanted to make you pregnant," he whispered, feeling her body jump as he said it. "And it scared me to death. You see, modern women don't want babies, because they're a trap. My mother taught me that."

Chapter 6

"That's not true!" She pressed closer. "I would have loved having a baby, and I'd never have felt trapped!" she said, her voice husky with feeling. Especially your baby, she added silently. "I didn't know any of your background, especially anything about your mother. You never told me."

His chest rose and fell abruptly. "I couldn't. You scared me to death. Maybe I deliberately upset you, to make you run. But when I got what I thought I wanted, I didn't want it. It hurt when you wouldn't even look at me, at the bus stop. I guess I'd shamed you so badly that you couldn't." He sighed. "I thought you were modern, that we'd enjoy each other and that would be the end of it. I got the shock of my life that last night. I couldn't even deal with it. I lost my head."

She lifted her face and looked into his eyes. "You

were honest about it. You'd already said that you wanted no part of marriage or a family, that all you could offer me was a night in your arms with no strings attached. But I couldn't manage to stop, or stop you, until the very last. I was raised to think of sleeping around as a sin.''

His face contorted. He averted his eyes to keep her from seeing the pain in them. ''I didn't know that until it was much too late. Sometimes, you don't realize how much things mean to you until you lose them.''

His fingers moved gently in her hair while she stood quietly, breathing uneasily. ''It wasn't just our mother who soured us on women. Simon was married,'' he said after a minute. ''He was the only one of us who ever was. His wife got pregnant the first time they were together, but she didn't want a child. She didn't really want Simon, she just wanted to be rich. He was crazy about her.'' He sighed painfully. ''She had an abortion and he found out later, accidentally. They had a fight on the way home from one of her incessant parties. He wrecked the car, she died and he lost an arm. That's why he doesn't live on the ranch. He can't do the things he used to do. He's embittered and he's withdrawn from the rest of us.'' He laughed a little. ''You think the four of us hate women. You should see Simon.''

She stirred in his arms. ''Poor man. He must have loved her very much.''

''Too much. That's another common problem we seem to have. We love irrationally and obsessively.''

''And reluctantly,'' she guessed.

He laughed. ''And that.''

He let her go with a long sigh and stared down at her warmly. "I suppose I'd better take you home. If you're still here when the boys get back, they'll tie you to the stove."

She smiled. "I like your brothers." She hesitated. "Corrigan, they aren't really going to try to force you to marry me, are they?"

"Of course not," he scoffed. "They're only teasing."

"Okay."

It was a good thing, he thought, that she couldn't see his fingers crossed behind his back.

He took her home, pausing to kiss her gently at the front door.

"I'll be along tomorrow night," he said softly. "We'll go to a movie. There's a new one every Saturday night at the Roxy downtown."

She searched his eyes and tried to decide if he was doing this because he wanted to or because his brothers were pestering him.

He smiled. "Don't worry so much. You're home, it's going to be Christmas, you have a job and plenty of friends. It's going to be the best Christmas you've ever had."

She smiled back. "Maybe it will be," she said, catching some of his own excitement. Her gaze caressed his face. They were much more like friends, with all the dark secrets out in the open. But his kisses had made her too hungry for him. She needed time to get her emotions under control. Perhaps a day would do it. He was throwing out broad hints of some sort, but he hadn't spoken one word of love. In that respect, nothing had changed.

"Good night, then," he said.

"Good night."

She closed the door and turned on the lights. It had been a strange and wonderful day. Somehow, the future looked unusually bright, despite all her worries.

The next morning, Dorie had to go into town to Clarisse's shop to help her with the bookkeeping. It was unfortunate that when she walked in, a beautiful woman in designer clothes should be standing at the counter, discussing Corrigan.

"It's going to be the most glorious Christmas ever!" she was telling the other woman, pushing back her red-gold hair and laughing. "Corrigan is taking me to the Christmas party at the Coltrains' house, and afterward we're going to Christmas Eve services at the Methodist Church." She sighed. "I'm glad to be home. You know, there's been some talk about Corrigan and a woman from his past who just came back recently. I asked him about it, if he was serious about her." She laughed gaily. "He said that he was just buttering her up so that she'd do some bookkeeping for him and the brothers, that she'd run out on him once and he didn't have any intention of letting her get close enough to do it again. I told him that I could find it in my heart to feel sorry for her, and he said that he didn't feel sorry for her at all, that he had plans for her..."

Clarisse spotted Dorie and caught her breath. "Why, Dorothy, I wasn't expecting you...quite so soon!"

"I thought I'd say hello," Dorie said, frozen in the

doorway. She managed a pasty smile. "I'll come back Monday. Have a nice weekend."

"Who was that?" she heard the other woman say as she went quickly back out the door and down the street to where she'd parked the car Turkey Sanders had returned early in the morning, very nicely fixed.

She got behind the wheel, her fingers turning white as she gripped it. She could barely see for the tears. She started the engine with shaking fingers and backed out into the street. She heard someone call to her and saw the redhead standing on the sidewalk, with an odd expression on her face, trying to get Dorie's attention.

She didn't look again. She put the car into gear and sped out of town.

She didn't go straight home. She went to a small park inside the city and sat down among the gay lights and decorations with a crowd that had gathered for a Christmas concert performed by the local high school band and chorus. There were so many people that one more didn't matter, and her tears weren't as noticeable in the crush of voices.

The lovely, familiar carols were oddly soothing. But her Christmas spirit was absent. How could she have trusted Corrigan? She was falling in love all over again, and he was setting her up for a fall. She'd never believe a word he said, ever again. And now that she'd had a look at his beautiful divorcée, she knew she wouldn't have a chance with him. That woman was exquisite, from her creamy skin to her perfect figure and face. The only surprising thing was that he hadn't married her years ago. Surely a woman like that wouldn't hang around waiting, when she could have any man she wanted.

Someone offered her a cup of hot apple cider, and she managed a smile and thanked the child who held it out to her. It was spicy and sweet and tasted good against the chill. She sipped it, thinking how horrible it was going to be from now on, living in Jacobsville with Corrigan only a few miles away and that woman hanging on his arm. He hadn't mentioned anything about Christmas to Dorie, but apparently he had his plans all mapped out if he was taking the merry divorcée to a party. When had he been going to tell her the truth? Or had he been going to let her find it out all for herself?

She couldn't remember ever feeling quite so bad. She finished the cider, listened to one more song and then got up and walked through the crowd, down the long sidewalk to where she'd parked her car. She sat in it for a moment, trying to decide what to do. It was Saturday and she had nothing planned for today. She wasn't going to go home. She couldn't bear the thought of going home.

She turned the car and headed up to the interstate, on the road to Victoria.

Corrigan paced up and down Dorie's front porch for an hour until he realized that she wasn't coming home. He drove back to town and pulled up in front of Tira Beck's brick house.

She came out onto the porch, in jeans and a sweatshirt, her glorious hair around her shoulders. Her arms were folded and she looked concerned. Her frantic phone call had sent him flying over to Dorie's house hours before he was due to pick her up for the movie. Now it looked as if the movie, and anything else, was off.

"Well?" she asked.

He shook his head, with his hands deep in his jacket pockets. "She wasn't there. I waited for an hour. There's no note on the door, no nothing."

Tira sighed miserably. "It's all my fault. Me and my big mouth. I had no idea who she was, and I didn't know that what I was telling Clarisse was just a bunch of bull that you'd handed me to keep me from seeing how much you cared for the woman." She looked up accusingly. "See what happens when you lie to your friends?"

"You didn't have to tell her that!"

"I didn't know she was there! And we had agreed to go to the Coltrains' party together, you and me and Charles Percy."

"You didn't mention that you had a date for it, I guess?" he asked irritably.

"No. I didn't realize anyone except Clarisse was listening, and she already knew I was going with Charles."

He tilted his hat further over his tired eyes. "God, the webs we weave," he said heavily. "She's gone and I don't know where to look for her. She might have gone back to New York for all I know, especially after yesterday. She had every reason to think I was dead serious about her until this morning."

Tira folded her arms closer against the cold look he shot her. "I said I'm sorry," she muttered. "I tried to stop her and tell her that she'd misunderstood me about the party, that I wasn't your date. But she wouldn't even look at me. I'm not sure she saw me. She was crying."

He groaned aloud.

"Oh, Corrigan, I'm sorry," she said gently. "Simon always says you do everything the hard way. I guess he knows you better than the others."

He glanced at her curiously. "When have you seen Simon?"

"At the cattle convention in San Antonio last week. I sold a lot of my Montana herd there."

"And he actually spoke to you?"

She smiled wistfully. "He always speaks to me," she said. "I don't treat him like an invalid. He feels comfortable with me."

He gave her an intent look. "He wouldn't if he knew how you felt about him."

Her eyes narrowed angrily. "I'm not telling him. And neither are you! If he wants me to be just a friend, I can settle for that. It isn't as if I'm shopping for a new husband. One was enough," she added curtly.

"Simon was always protective about you," he recalled. "Even before you married."

"He pushed me at John," she reminded him.

"Simon was married when he met you."

Her expression closed. She didn't say a word, but it was there, in her face. She'd hated Simon's wife, and the feeling had been mutual. Simon had hated her husband, too. But despite all the turbulence between Tira and Simon, there had never been a hint of infidelity while they were both married. Now, it was as if they couldn't get past their respective bad marriages to really look at each other romantically. Tira loved

Simon, although no one except Corrigan knew it. But
Simon kept secrets. No one was privy to them anymore, not even his own brothers. He kept to himself
in San Antonio. Too much, sometimes.

Tira was watching him brood. "Why don't you file
a missing persons report?" she suggested suddenly.

"I have to wait twenty-four hours. She could be in
Alaska by then." He muttered under his breath. "I
guess I could hire a private detective to look for her."

She gave him a thoughtful look and her eyes twin-
kled. "I've got a better idea. Why not tell your brothers she's gone missing?"

His eyebrows lifted, and hope returned. "Now
that's a constructive suggestion," he agreed, nodding,
and he began to grin. "They were already looking
forward to homemade biscuits every morning. They'll
be horrified!"

And they were. It was amazing, the looks that he
got from his own kinfolk when he mentioned that
their prized biscuit maker had gone missing.

"It's your fault," Rey said angrily. "You should
have proposed to her."

"I thought you guys had all that taken care of,"
Corrigan said reasonably. "The rings, the minister,
the gown, the invitations…"

"Everything except the most important part," Cag
told him coldly.

"Oh, that. Did we forget to tell her that he loved
her?" Leo asked sharply. "Good Lord, we did! No
wonder she left!" He glared at his brother. "You
could have told her yourself if you hadn't been chewing on your hurt pride. And speaking of pride, why

didn't you tell Tira the truth instead of hedging your bets with a bunch of lies?''

"Because Tira has a big mouth and I didn't want the whole town to know I was dying of unrequited love for Dorie!" he raged. "She doesn't want to marry me. She said so! A man has to have a little pride to cling to!"

"Pride and those sort of biscuits don't mix," Rey stressed. "We've got to get her back. Okay, boys, who do we know in the highway patrol? Better yet, don't we know at least one Texas Ranger? Those boys can track anybody! Let's pool resources here…"

Watching them work, Corrigan felt relieved for himself and just a little sorry for Dorie. She wouldn't stand a chance.

She didn't, either. A tall, good-looking man with black hair wearing a white Stetson and a Texas Ranger's star on his uniform knocked at the door of her motel room in Victoria. When she answered it, he tipped his hat politely, smiled and put her in handcuffs.

They were halfway back to Jacobsville, her hastily packed suitcase and her purse beside her, before she got enough breath back to protest.

"But why have you arrested me?" she demanded.

"Why?" He thought for a minute and she saw him scowl in the rearview mirror. "Oh, I remember. Cattle rustling." He nodded. "Yep, that's it. Cattle rustling." He glanced at her in the rearview mirror. "You see, rustling is a crime that cuts across county lines, which gave me the authority to arrest you."

"Whose cattle have I rustled?" she demanded impertinently.

"The Hart Brothers filed the charges."

"Hart…Corrigan Hart?" She made a furious sound under her breath. "No. Not Corrigan. Them. It was them! Them and their damned biscuits! It's a put-up job," she exclaimed. "They've falsely accused me so that they can get me back into their kitchen!"

He chuckled at the way she phrased it. The Hart brothers and their mania for biscuits was known far and wide. "No, ma'am, I can swear to that," he told her. His twinkling black eyes shone out of a lean, darkly tanned face. His hair was black, too, straight and thick under that wide-brimmed white hat. "They showed me where it was."

"It?"

"The bull you rustled. His stall was empty, all right."

Her eyes bulged. "Didn't you look for him on the ranch?"

"Yes, ma'am," he assured her with a wide smile. "I looked. But the stall was empty, and they said he'd be in it if he hadn't been rustled. That was a million-dollar bull, ma'am." He shook his head. "They could shoot you for that. This is Texas, you know. Cattle rustling is a very serious charge."

"How could I rustle a bull? Do you have any idea how much a bull weighs?" She was sounding hysterical. She calmed down. "All right. If I took that bull, where was he?"

"Probably hidden in your room, ma'am. I plan to phone back when we get to the Hart place and have the manager search it," he assured her. His rakish grin widened. "Of course, if he doesn't find a bull in your room, that will probably mean that I can drop the charges."

"Drop them, the devil!" she flared, blowing a wisp of platinum hair out of her eyes. "I'll sue the whole damned state for false arrest!"

He chuckled at her fury. "Sorry. You can't. I had probable cause."

"What probable cause?"

He glanced at her in the rearview mirror with a rakish grin. "You had a hamburger for lunch, didn't you, ma'am?"

She was openly gasping by now. The man was a lunatic. He must be a friend of the brothers, that was the only possible explanation. She gave up arguing, because she couldn't win. But she was going to do some serious damage to four ugly men when she got back to Jacobsville.

The ranger pulled up in front of the Harts' ranch house and all four of them came tumbling out of the living room and down to the driveway. Every one of them was smiling except Corrigan.

"Thanks, Colton," Leo said, shaking the ranger's hand. "I don't know what we'd have done without you."

The man called Colton got out and opened the back seat to extricate a fuming, muttering Dorie. She glared at the brothers with eyes that promised retribution as her handcuffs were removed and her suitcase and purse handed to her.

"We found the bull," Cag told the ranger. "He'd strayed just out behind the barn. Sorry to have put you to this trouble. We'll make our own apologies to Miss Wayne, here.''

Colton stared at the fuming ex-prisoner with pursed lips. ''Good luck,'' he told them.

Dorie didn't know where to start. She looked up at Colton and wondered how many years she could get for kicking a Texas Ranger's shin.

Reading that intent in her eyes, he chuckled and climbed back into his car. ''Tell Simon I said hello,'' he called to them. ''We miss seeing him around the state capital now that he's given up public office.''

''I'll tell him,'' Cag promised.

That barely registered as he drove away with a wave of his hand, leaving Dorie alone with the men.

''Nice to see you again, Miss Wayne,'' Cag said, tipping his hat. ''Excuse me. Cows to feed.''

''Fences to mend,'' Leo added, grinning as he followed Cag's example.

''Right. Me, too.'' Rey tipped his own hat and lit out after his brothers.

Which left Corrigan to face the music, and it was all furious discord and bass.

She folded her arms over her breasts and glared at him.

''It was their idea,'' he said pointedly.

''Arrested for rustling. Me! He…that man…that Texas Ranger tried to infer that I had a bull hidden in my motel room, for God's sake! He handcuffed me!'' She held up her wrists to show them to him.

''He probably felt safer that way,'' he remarked, observing her high color and furious face.

''I want to go home! Right now!''

He could see that it would be useless to try to talk

to her. He only made one small effort. "Tira's sorry," he said quietly. "She wanted to tell you that she's going to the Coltrains' party with Charles Percy. I was going to drive, that's all. I'd planned to take you with me."

"I heard all about your 'plan.'"

The pain in her eyes was hard to bear. He averted his gaze. "You'd said repeatedly that you wanted no part of me," he said curtly. "I wasn't about to let people think I was dying of love for you."

"Wouldn't that be one for the record books?" she said furiously.

His gaze met hers evenly. "I'll get Joey to drive you home."

He turned and walked away, favoring his leg a little. She watched him with tears in her eyes. It was just too much for one weekend.

Joey drove her home and she stayed away from the ranch. Corrigan was back to doing the books himself, because she wouldn't. Her pride was raw, and so was his. It looked like a complete stalemate.

"We've got to do something," Cag said on Christmas Eve, as Corrigan sat in the study all by himself in the dark. "It's killing him. He won't even talk about going to the Coltrains' party."

"I'm not missing it," Leo said. "They've got five sets of Lionel electric trains up and running on one of the most impressive layouts in Texas."

"Your brother is more important than trains," Rey said grimly. "What are we going to do?"

Cag's dark eyes began to twinkle. "I think we should bring him a Christmas present."

"What sort of present?" Rey asked.

"A biscuit maker," Cag said.

Leo chuckled. "I'll get a bow."

"I'll get out the truck," Rey said, shooting out the front door.

"Shhh!" Cag called to them. "It wouldn't do to let him know what we're up to. We've already made one monumental mistake."

They nodded and moved more stealthily.

Corrigan was nursing a glass of whiskey. He heard the truck leave and come back about an hour later, but he wasn't really interested in what his brothers were doing. They'd probably gone to the Christmas party over at Coltrain's ranch.

He was still sitting in the dark when he heard curious muffled sounds and a door closing.

He got up and went out into the hall. His brothers looked flushed and flustered and a little mussed. They looked at him, wide-eyed. Leo was breathing hard, leaning against the living-room door.

"What are you three up to now?" he demanded.

"We put your Christmas present in there," Leo said, indicating the living room. "We're going to let you open it early."

"It's something nice," Cag told him.

"And very useful," Leo agreed.

Rey heard muffled noises getting louder. "Better let him get in there. I don't want to have to run it down again."

"Run it down?" Corrigan cocked his head. "What the hell have you got in there? Not another rattler...!"

"Oh, it's not that dangerous," Cag assured him.

He frowned. "Well, not quite that dangerous." He moved forward, extricated Leo from the door and opened it, pushing Corrigan inside. "Merry Christmas," he added, and locked the door.

Corrigan noticed two things at once—that the door was locked, and that a gunnysack tied with a ribbon was sitting in a chair struggling like crazy.

Outside the door, there were muffled voices.

"Oh, God," he said apprehensively.

He untied the red ribbon that had the top securely tied, and out popped a raging mad Dorothy Wayne.

"I'll kill them!" she yelled.

Big booted feet ran for safety out in the hall.

Corrigan started laughing and couldn't stop. Honest to God, his well-meaning brothers were going to be the death of him.

"I hate them, I hate this ranch, I hate Jacobsville, I hate you...*mmmfff!*"

He stopped the furious tirade with his mouth. Amazing how quickly she calmed down when his arms went around her and he eased her gently out of the chair and down onto the long leather couch.

She couldn't get enough breath to continue. His mouth was open and hungry on her lips and his body was as hard as hers was soft as it moved restlessly against her.

She felt his hands on her hips and, an instant later, he was lying between her thighs, moving in a tender, achingly soft rhythm that made her moan.

"I love you," he whispered before she could get a word out.

And then she didn't want to get a word out.

His hands were inside her blouse and he was fighting his way under her skirt when they dimly heard a key turn in the lock.

The door opened and three pair of shocked, delighted eyes peered in.

"You monsters!" she said with the last breath she had. She was in such a state of disarray that she couldn't manage anything else. Their position was so blatant that there was little use in pretending that they were just talking.

"That's no way to talk to your brothers-in-law," Leo stated. "The wedding's next Saturday, by the way." He smiled apologetically. "We couldn't get the San Antonio symphony orchestra to come, because they have engagements, but we did get the governor to give you away. He'll be along just before the ceremony." He waved a hand at them and grinned. "Carry on, don't mind us."

Corrigan fumbled for a cushion and flung it with all his might at the door. It closed. Outside, deep chuckles could be heard.

Dorie looked up into Corrigan's steely gray eyes with wonder. "Did he say the governor's going to give me away? Our governor? The governor of Texas?"

"The very one."

"But, how?"

"The governor's a friend of ours. Simon worked with him until the wreck, when he retired from public office. Don't you ever read a newspaper?"

"I guess not."

"Never mind. Just forget about all the details." He bent to her mouth. "Now, where were we...?"

* * *

The wedding was the social event of the year. The governor did give her away; along with all four brothers, including the tall, darkly distinguished Simon, who wore an artificial arm just for the occasion. Dorie was exquisite in a Paris gown designed especially for her by a well-known couturier. Newspapers sent representatives. The whole world seemed to form outside the little Presbyterian church in Victoria.

"I can't believe this," she whispered to Corrigan as they were leaving on their Jamaica honeymoon. "Corrigan, that's the vice president over there, standing beside the governor and Simon!"

"Well, they sort of want Simon for a cabinet position. He doesn't want to leave Texas. They're coaxing him."

She just shook her head. The Hart family was just too much altogether!

That night, lying in her new husband's arms with the sound of the ocean right outside the window, she gazed up at him with wonder as he made the softest, sweetest love to her in the dimly lit room.

His body rose and fell like the tide, and he smiled at her, watching her excited eyes with sparks in his own as her body hesitated only briefly and then accepted him completely on a gasp of shocked pleasure.

"And you were afraid that it was going to hurt," he chided as he moved tenderly against her.

"Yes." She was gasping for air, clinging, lifting to him in shivering arcs of involuntary rigor. "It's...killing me...!"

"Already?" he chided, bending to brush his lips

over her swollen mouth. "Darlin', we've barely started!"

"Barely...? Oh!"

He was laughing. She could hear him as she washed up and down on waves of ecstasy that brought unbelievable noises out of her. She died half a dozen times, almost lost consciousness, and still he laughed, deep in his throat, as he went from one side of the bed to the other with her in a tangle of glorious abandon that never seemed to end. Eventually they ended up on the carpet with the sheet trailing behind them as she cried out, sobbing, one last time and heard him groan as he finally shuddered to completion.

They were both covered with sweat. Her hair was wet. She was trembling and couldn't stop. Beside her, he lay on his back with one leg bent at the knee. Incredibly he was still as aroused as he'd been when they started. She sat up gingerly and stared at him, awed.

He chuckled up at her. "Come down here," he dared her.

"I can't!" She was gasping. "And you can't...you couldn't...!"

"If you weren't the walking wounded, I sure as hell could," he said. "I've saved it all up for eight years, and I'm still starving for you."

She just looked at him, fascinated. "I read a book."

"I'm not in it," he assured her. He tugged her down on top of him and brushed her breasts with his lips. "I guess you're sore."

She blushed. "You *guess?*"

He chuckled. "All right. Come here, my new best

friend, and we'll go to sleep, since we can't do anything else.''

''We're on the floor,'' she noted.

''At least we won't fall off next time.''

She laughed because he was outrageous. She'd never thought that intimacy would be fun as well as pleasurable. She traced his nose and bent to kiss his lips. ''Where are we going to live?''

''At the ranch.''

''Only if your brothers live in the barn,'' she said. ''I'm not having them outside the door every night listening to us.''

''They won't have to stand outside the door. Judging from what I just heard, they could hear you with the windows closed if they stood on the town squa… Ouch!''

''Let that be a lesson to you,'' she told him dryly, watching him rub the nip she'd given his thigh. ''Naked men are vulnerable.''

''And you aren't?''

''Now, Corrigan…!''

She screeched and he laughed and they fell down again in a tangle, close together, and the laughter gave way to soft conversation. Eventually they even slept.

When they got back to the ranch, the three brothers were gone and there was a hastily scrawled note on the door.

''We're sleeping in the bunkhouse until we can build you a house of your own. Congratulations. Champagne is in the fridge.'' It was signed with love, all three brothers—and the name of the fourth was penciled in.

''On second thought,'' she said, with her arm

around her husband, ''maybe those boys aren't so bad after all!''

He tried to stop her from opening the door, but it was too late. The bucket of water left her wavy hair straight and her navy blue coat dripping. She looked at Corrigan with eyes the size of plates, her arms outstretched, her mouth open.

Corrigan looked around her. On the floor of the hall were two towels and two new bathrobes, and an assortment of unmentionable items.

He knew that if he laughed, he'd be sleeping in the barn for the next month. But he couldn't help it. And after a glance at the floor—neither could she.

*   *   *   *   *

*Don't miss Diana Palmer's
next Silhouette Romance—
it's coming your way in March 1998!*

**Turn the Page for a
Special Holiday Interview
with Bestselling Author
Diana Palmer**

A Conversation with Diana Palmer

Q. How did you get started writing?

A. "I got started writing because I spent so much time daydreaming that it seemed a shame not to try and make a living at it. And I was never cut out for a nine-to-five job."

Q. What is your favorite aspect of writing? Do you have a favorite time of day to write?

A. "Research. I love to learn new things and stick tidbits of factual information in my books. I like to write late at night because everybody who calls me thinks I'm asleep. I do write during the day as well, but the telephone worries me to death."

Q. What does Christmas mean to you?

A. "It means having time to spend with my family and enjoying the Christmas tree and the special foods and the magical atmosphere of the season. God opens the heart at Christmas and pours in an extra helping of love."

Q. Do you have a favorite holiday story?

A. "My favorite Christmas story is, and always has been, Charles Dickens' *A Christmas Carol*. Nothing expresses the special meaning of the holiday season like this wonderful work."

Q. What was the best Christmas gift you ever received?

A. "The best gift I ever received was having my husband alive to celebrate last Christmas with me. He had to have emergency open-heart surgery in February of 1996, and it is a true miracle that he is still here. If it had not been for our local hospital and Dr. Sanders, Dr. Stebbins and Dr. Bray, and in Atlanta at St. Joseph's Hospital, Dr. Carabajal, the heart surgeon; Dr. Gandy, the cardiologist; and Dr. Haynes, the pulmonary specialist; and the staffs of both hospitals, James would not be alive today. I would rather have my husband than any gift, of any kind, in the whole world."

Q. What's at the top of your Christmas list this year?

A. "A classical guitar. I bought a Harmony guitar with my first month's paycheck when I was eighteen. The guitar was accidentally broken last year. I searched the Internet for information and ended up with a fairly inexpensive but wonderful instrument called an Amanda. In Spanish, this means beloved—and to anyone who plays and loves the guitar, the name is quite appropriate. It sings like an angel."

Q. Do you have any family holiday traditions you practice every year?

A. "Our only real holiday tradition is that we put up the tree and all the exterior holiday lights so that we can light them simultaneously with the lighting of The Great Tree at Rich's Department Store in downtown Atlanta. The tree lighting at Rich's has been the highlight of the holidays for me since I was a small girl growing up in Atlanta."

Q. Do you have a holiday message for your readers?

A. "Life is too short to waste being angry at other people, regardless of the reason. Christmas challenges us to mete out unconditional love and unconditional forgiveness–difficult goals, but worth striving to achieve."

"I wish you all the merriest of Christmas seasons."

Diana Palmer

A HAWK'S WAY CHRISTMAS

JOAN JOHNSTON

For my mom,
who taught me the true meaning of Christmas.

And for my children,
who light up my life all year round.

Hawk's Way Family Tree

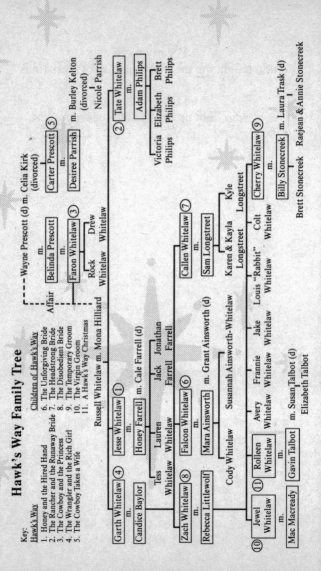

Key:

Hawk's Way
1. Honey and the Hired Hand
2. The Rancher and the Runaway Bride
3. The Cowboy and the Princess
4. The Wrangler and the Rich Girl
5. The Cowboy Takes a Wife

Children of Hawk's Way
6. The Unforgiving Bride
7. The Headstrong Bride
8. The Disobedient Bride
9. The Temporary Groom
10. The Virgin Groom
11. A Hawk's Way Christmas

Wayne Prescott (d) m. Celia Kirk (divorced)

Carter Prescott ⑤
m.
Desiree Parrish

Belinda Prescott
m.
Faron Whitelaw ③
Rock Whitelaw   Drew Whitelaw

Tate Whitelaw ②
m.
Burley Kelton (divorced)
Nicole Parrish

Adam Philips   Brett Philips

Victoria Philips   Elizabeth Philips

Russell Whitelaw m. Mona Hilliard

Jesse Whitelaw ① m. Honey Farrell m. Cale Farrell (d)
Tess Whitelaw   Lauren Whitelaw   Jack Farrell   Jonathan Farrell

Falcon Whitelaw ⑥ m. Mara Ainsworth m. Grant Ainsworth (d)
Cody Whitelaw   Susannah Ainsworth-Whitelaw

Callen Whitelaw ⑦ m. Sam Longstreet
Karen & Kayla Longstreet   Kyle Longstreet

Garth Whitelaw ④
m.
Candice Baylor

Zach Whitelaw ⑧
m.
Rebecca Littlewolf

Avery Whitelaw   Frannie Whitelaw   Jake Whitelaw   Louis "Rabbit" Whitelaw   Colt Whitelaw

Cherry Whitelaw ⑨ m. Billy Stonecreek m. Laura Trask (d)
Brett Stonecreek   Raejean & Annie Stonecreek

Rolleen Whitelaw ⑪ m. Gavin Talbot
Jewel Whitelaw ⑩ m. Mac Macready m. Susan Talbot (d)
Elizabeth Talbot

Chapter 1

Gavin Talbot had just stepped off the elevator and started down the hall of the pediatric wing of Houston Regional Hospital, when he thought he heard someone sobbing in the linen closet. He stopped and stared at the closed door. It was nearly midnight, and Gavin had decided he was so tired he was delusional, when he heard the sound again. Definitely sobbing. Female sobbing.

Gavin rapped his knuckles twice on the linen closet door. "Is somebody in there?"

"Go away," a tear-choked voice replied.

Gavin wished he were interning as a heart surgeon or an orthopedist. Those exhausted physicians wouldn't have had any trouble walking away. But he was studying to become a child psychologist, and he knew a cry for help when he heard one.

"Hey," he said. "Maybe I can help."

"No one can help," the tear-choked voice replied.

"How about opening the door?"

"Go away and leave me alone."

"I can't do that. Look, it's late. Why not have a cup of coffee with me in the cafeteria? Maybe we can work things out."

"You don't even know what the problem is!" an exasperated voice replied.

"I'm a good listener," he said. "Why don't you tell me?"

Absolute silence. He figured she was thinking about it. Gavin said nothing, just waited patiently and was rewarded when the door inched open and a swollen-eyed, tearstained face peeked out.

"How do I know you're not a serial killer?"

He held his hands wide, letting her get a good look at the wrinkled blue oxford-cloth shirt, the sleeves casually folded up to reveal muscular forearms, and the frayed, beltless Levi's he wore to make the kids he worked with feel more comfortable. "No gun, no knife, not even a needle. My name's Gavin Talbot. I'm working at the hospital on a research grant."

She opened the linen closet door wider, but hesitated on the threshold. He noticed her shoulder-length blond hair was cut in a fringe around her face, and she had pale, red-rimmed gray eyes that looked as desolate as any of the dying children he had ever counseled at the hospital.

Her shapeless dress was topped by a white hospital lab coat, identifying her as a medical student, and Gavin made an informed—and intuitive—guess about her situation.

Medical students were notoriously overworked and

under tremendous stress to perform at high levels, and fatigue and depression were common. She fit the profile. Dark circles played under her eyes, and her short frame was so delicate she looked fragile, like she would break if he were to hold her in his strong arms.

"I'm R. J. Whitelaw," she said, extending her hand. It held a wadded-up Kleenex. She quickly stuffed the tissue into her lab coat pocket and extended the hand again.

Gavin swallowed her small hand in his and was startled by her firm grip. It conveyed confidence and self-assurance; there was nothing the least bit fragile about it. "It's nice to meet you, R.J.," he said. "I know some Whitelaws, Zach and Rebecca. They own a ranch in northwest Texas called Hawk's Pride. Any relation?"

Her lips curved in a wobbly smile that cracked as she broke down and sobbed, "My par-hents."

"I don't recognize R.J. as one of their kids' names," he said.

"I'm Ro-hol-le-heen."

She groped for her Kleenex, and he handed her the hanky from his back Levi's pocket. "Try this."

"Tha-hanks," she said, then blew her nose noisily.

"You don't remember me, do you?"

Her brow wrinkled as she rubbed at her reddened nose. "Should I?"

"We spoke on the phone. Your sister Jewel asked me to get in touch with you after I spent last summer as a counselor at Camp LittleHawk."

"Oh, no!" Her gray eyes filled to the brim with tears that quickly spilled over. "You ca-han't tell her you saw me li-hike this."

"I promise not to do that," Gavin said, taking Rolleen's arm and heading her toward the cafeteria. "Let's go get that coffee and find a quiet place to talk."

Camp LittleHawk, a camp for kids with cancer located on the Whitelaws' northwest Texas ranch, had been started by Rolleen's mother Rebecca and was now run by Rolleen's sister Jewel. Gavin had met most of the Whitelaw clan over the summer, when he'd worked at the camp, and had promised Jewel he would look up her sister Rolleen when he got back to Houston.

And he had. He and Rolleen had traded phone messages several times, but they'd both been so busy, he'd given up trying to get together with her. Now he'd met her, and Gavin was suddenly a lot more than a detached observer of someone in trouble.

He knew Rolleen was the eldest of the eight Whitelaw kids. And smart. "Rolleen's away at medical school," Rebecca had told him proudly. "She's been at the top of her class during each of the past two years."

Obviously something had gone very wrong. He wondered if she was having trouble keeping up her grades, and if so, why.

When they reached the cafeteria, the door was locked and all the lights were out. Gavin looked at his watch and made a disgusted sound. "I forgot the cafeteria closes at midnight over the holidays."

"I wasn't thinking, either." Rolleen disengaged her arm from his and said, "Thanks anyway for the offer."

She had already turned to leave when Gavin caught

her by the shoulder. "Wait. Why don't we go across the street to the Coffee Caper? They're open twenty-four hours a day."

She wiped at the tears on her cheeks with the heel of her hand, shook her head, then looked up at him with those desolate gray eyes. "I don't want anyone to see me looking like this."

"There must be someplace we can go to talk," he said. "Your place? Or mine?"

She looked at him askance. "I'm not in the habit of inviting strangers home with me—or going home with them."

He smiled his most trustworthy smile and said, "I'm not a stranger. I spent the entire summer working for your sister. I'm sure if you gave Jewel a call, she'd be willing to vouch for me."

Rolleen visibly shuddered. "No. I don't want to speak to her—to any of them—right now. They'd know...they'd know..."

When tears began to spill from her eyes again, he simply pulled her toward him—tugging when she at first resisted—put his arms around her and hugged her gently, aware of his much greater size and strength.

She gripped him tightly around the waist while she cried, as though if she didn't, she would fly away into pieces. The strength of her hold on him once again contradicted his fragile image of her. There was nothing delicate about her crying, either. Her whole body heaved with sobs so painful they made his throat ache—and he didn't even know what her problem was.

Yet she hadn't collapsed entirely. She was still

standing on her own two feet. There was plainly more to R. J. Whitelaw than met the eye.

When the sobbing had resolved into hiccups, Gavin kept one arm around Rolleen and began walking her down the deserted hall toward his mentor's office, where he'd been headed in the first place. He got out his key and unlocked the door and eased her inside. When he reached for the light, her hand was there to stop him.

"Don't. I look awful."

If she was able to think about how she looked, she was feeling better, Gavin thought. The light streaming in from the hall through the old-fashioned, half-shuttered venetian blinds was enough for them to see each other's faces, and she was right about her appearance. Her eyes and nose were puffy and swollen and red.

"All right," he conceded. "No light. Why don't you sit down and take it easy?" He eased her onto the well-used black leather couch and felt her tense as he sat down beside her. He put more distance between them and heard her exhale in a relieved sigh.

She rested her elbows on her knees and dropped her face into her hands. He didn't resist the urge to put a comforting hand on her shoulder and rub at what turned out to be very tense muscles on her shoulders and neck.

"That feels wonderful," she said.

"Let's get rid of this," he said, easing off her lab coat. He angled her slightly away, so he could use both hands effectively, and said, "You want to tell me about it?"

"There's nothing you can do to help," she said resignedly.

"What have you got to lose by telling me?"

She sighed again. "Nothing, I suppose."

Between the softness of her skin, the small, enticing curls on her nape and the little sounds of pleasure she was making, Gavin realized he was becoming aroused in the seductive darkness. He stopped what he was doing and slid back across the couch.

He leaned forward, draping his arms on his widespread thighs, and said, "I'm listening, Rolleen, if you'd like to talk."

"I've been using R.J. at school," she said. "I think it sounds more—never mind."

More what? Gavin wondered. But he didn't ask. He was merely providing a friendly shoulder for the sister of a friend. "Rolleen's what I've heard you called all summer," he said. "It's unusual and pretty—like you."

She started to speak, stopped herself, then said, "Rolleen's fine."

He had a feeling it wasn't really fine, but he didn't want to get sidetracked talking about her name when something much more important was bothering her. "All right, Rolleen," he said. "Shoot."

She hesitated as though on a high diving board, her face thoughtful, then dove in. "If you've met my parents you know they think I'm the perfect daughter."

"I don't think I heard a disparaging word about you all summer," he admitted with a smile. "And praise was heaped on your head."

She made a face. "That's the problem. I've always been the 'good little girl.'"

"Really? How come?"

"Because by the time Zach and Rebecca adopted me from the Good Souls Orphanage I'd made a promise to God that if He sent somebody to take me out of that place, I'd repay Him by being the best daughter any parents could ever have."

Gavin realized he was hearing the truth and was humbled by it. "It sounds like you kept your promise."

Her mouth shifted in a crooked smile. "Pretty much. I stole some gum once from the five-and-dime in town—to see if I could get away with it." Her lips quirked as she admitted, "I didn't. And I got caught smoking once in the high school bathroom. But I was a straight-A student and president of the student council and a soloist with the church choir and helpful around the house. And a devoted daughter."

She looked up at him, and the grief and despair were back in her eyes. "That's why what's happened is so awful. Momma and Daddy are going to be so disappointed in me when they find out what I've done."

Her eyes began misting again, and he reminded her, "You still haven't told me what it is you've done that's so bad you don't want your family finding out about it."

She stood slowly and turned in profile, then pressed her hands along the front of her dress from the waist downward. He saw the slight outward curve of her belly, and felt his stomach turn over. *She's pregnant.*

"I'm pregnant," she said.

He stood, crossed away from her to the desk and settled his hip on the corner, trying to be nonchalant.

But he knew the Whitelaws well enough to know they *would* be disappointed in their daughter, of whom they were so proud. "Who's the father?" he asked. "And where is he?"

"One of my professors," she replied. "He's spending the next year at the Centers for Disease Control in Atlanta, completing a study on viruses."

"Does he know about the baby?"

"Yes."

"And?"

"He said the problem is mine, and that I should solve it. Meaning, I should get an abortion," she said bitterly. "Or give up the baby for adoption."

"Those are available options," he said neutrally.

"Not for me! I'm going to have this baby and keep it and love it enough for both parents!"

She slumped back onto the couch. "But I'm going to have to quit medical school to do it. I can't ask my parents to support me and a child, too. That wouldn't be fair to them."

"Don't you think that ought to be their decision?"

"I know they wouldn't begrudge me the money," she said. "But I can't take advantage of them like that. After everything they've done for me, look how I've repaid them—by getting pregnant without a husband, without even a fiancé!"

She took a hitching breath and blew it out. "I'm sorry. I shouldn't be burdening you with my problems." She walked past him to stare out through the half-open venetian blinds, her arms crossed protectively over her small bosom. "I dread spoiling everyone's Christmas when I go home next Tuesday. I'd stay here, but then they'd know something was wrong and come after me.''

She turned to face him. "Christmas has always been a special time of year for my family. On Christmas Eve, Momma always tells the story of how she met and married Daddy, and how together they picked each one of us to be the family Momma could never bear in her womb…"

Her face was crumpling again, and he quickly asked, "How will they know you're pregnant, if you don't tell them?"

"The eight of us kids have always shared bedrooms. It's hard to keep secrets when you share a double bed," she said, managing a brittle smile. "I'll be four months pregnant by Christmas, and I'll be dressing and undressing in front of my sisters. They'll surely notice my figure has changed."

"I see."

"Even if I could hide in the bathroom to dress, I've never worn blousy clothes, so that would be a tip-off. And if I tried wearing jeans…" She turned and held her dress tight against her slim figure—slim except for the bulge in the middle. "They'll see the truth for themselves. And my family is so physical—rambunctious, playful, ripping and tearing around the house, horseback riding at a full gallop, flag football that ends up being full tackle—they'd know the instant I excused myself from any of those activities that something was up."

"You do seem to have a problem," Gavin murmured.

Her chin began to quiver. "Momma will cry when she finds out. And Daddy…he'll get quiet as a sunset on the prairie. But I'll know he's feeling bad, because it'll be right there in his eyes. He's no poker player, my dad.''

She swallowed hard before she said, ''They'll be so unhappy, it'll spoil Christmas for the whole family. And that'll be one more thing I'll have to feel guilty about.''

Her chin was still quivering, but she had her teeth clenched to keep from losing control. He was pretty sure an iron rod ran down Ms. Whitelaw's slender back.

''I don't know what I'm going to do,'' she said unhappily.

Respecting that inner core of strength—and the pride that had put it there—Gavin resisted the urge to offer platitudes. He wanted to help her, but he wasn't sure what he could do. He had little personal experience to draw on. The rollicking Christmas she had described was nothing like what Christmas had been for him in the past, or was going to be like for him this year.

He had come from a small family, an only child of parents who had died in a private plane crash when he was eleven, and he had a small family of his own—himself, his four-year-old daughter Beth and his grandmother Hester. This was the first Christmas since his wife, Susan, had died. Or, more precisely, since Susan had committed suicide, scrawling a note that said nothing about why she had taken her own life, but telling him that Beth was not his child.

Gavin had spent the past year tortured by thoughts of the woman he'd loved in another man's arms. Wondering endlessly why Susan had killed herself.

Wondering what he had done to make his wife betray him. And furious at the thought that his precious daughter, whom he had adored, was not his own flesh and blood. He had become a distant parent to his child, unable to hug her and love her the way he had before Susan's revelation.

Gavin was certain his grandmother was planning to manipulate things so he ended up spending a lot of time over the Christmas holiday with Beth. Hester firmly believed that time and proximity would wear down his reserve.

But she was wrong. Ever since he had read Susan's note, he hadn't been able to look at his daughter without feeling physically ill. He couldn't bear to disappoint Hester by staying away at Christmas—he wasn't sure how many Christmases his grandmother had left—but he had been desperately searching for a way to avoid being alone with Beth.

Gavin looked up and met Rolleen's grim, gray-eyed gaze. "I may have a solution to your problem," he said tentatively.

Her brows rose in question.

"This may sound a bit farfetched, but hear me out before you say no," he said.

"All right."

"I think we should get engaged."

Rolleen backed up against the door and stared at him wide-eyed. "What?"

He rose and came toward her, but when she reached for the doorknob, he stopped and held out his hands placatingly. "Don't leave. Please just listen."

"I'm listening."

"What I'm suggesting is a temporary, make-believe engagement,'' Gavin said, warming up to his subject as he realized what a good idea it was. ''When you go home for Christmas, I'll go with you. You'll still be pregnant and unmarried, of course, but you'll have a doting fiancé on your arm. We'll tell your parents there are practical reasons why we can't marry now, but we plan to marry before the baby's born.''

''What reasons?'' Rolleen said. When he frowned she explained, ''They'll want to know why we aren't married.''

''I'm sure we can come up with some good excuses,'' he said. ''What do you think?''

''It's not a bad idea,'' she said, ''but I couldn't let you—''

''I'm not doing this only as a favor to you. I want something in return.''

Her eyes narrowed. ''I'm listening.''

''We can spend the holiday until Christmas Eve at your family's ranch, but I want you to come to my house on Christmas Day and spend the rest of the holiday there.''

A pinched V appeared at the bridge of her nose. ''Why?''

''It's a long story, and I've got two weeks before Christmas to tell you all about it. Suffice it to say, I'll play your fiancé and you'll play mine for the duration of the holidays.''

''We don't even know each other!''

''But we have an excuse for knowing each other. It was your sister Jewel who arranged the introduction by asking me to look you up in August—about four months ago,'' he pointed out, letting her see how easy it would be to carry out the deception.

''I don't know anything about you,'' Rolleen said. ''We'd never be able to fool my family. They'd know right away we were strangers.''

''Not if we spend the next ten days getting to know each other,'' Gavin argued.

Rolleen pursed her lips. ''I still won't have solved the problem of telling my parents I'm going to be a single mother.''

''No, but you'll have saved Christmas for everybody. After you've been back at school for a while, you can call or write your parents and say we've broken up.''

Rolleen folded her hands together behind her back and wandered past him to the other side of the room, examined an autographed Cal Ripken, Jr. baseball in a hermetically sealed case on the credenza, then meandered back to the door. She turned to face him and said, ''I suppose it might work.''

''It'll work, all right,'' Gavin said, thinking how agreeable his grandmother would be when he asked her to keep Beth while he had some grown-up time with his fiancée. Hester would be glad to see him happy again and downright ecstatic at the thought he might marry and provide her with more grandchildren. Rolleen's presence would provide a welcome distraction on all counts.

''How do you propose we get to know each other?'' Rolleen asked.

''We're going to have to spend some time together, at my place, at yours, kissing, touching—''

"Whoa, there! Hold your horses!" Rolleen said. "Kissing and touching?"

Gavin shrugged. "I don't know any engaged couples who don't kiss and touch. Do you?"

He watched as Rolleen scratched the back of her neck, and recalled the enticing curls on her nape. He might be kissing her there sometime soon, he realized in amazement.

"I hadn't figured on getting intimate with another man," she said thoughtfully.

"I'm not suggesting we go to bed together," Gavin said, "although, if you have any birthmarks I should know about—"

"I see your point," she interrupted. "And my family *will* expect us to kiss and hold hands."

"And touch," Gavin said. "Don't forget I've met them."

She wrinkled her nose like a kid facing a plateful of lima beans and spinach and brussels sprouts. "Within reason," she conceded.

"All right, then. We're agreed?"

"Agreed," Rolleen said, extending her hand.

Her hand and wrist were fragile, he realized, but the woman extending them wasn't. He was glad she had a strong backbone. She was going to need it to stand up to the interrogation his grandmother was certain to give her. All in all, Gavin was satisfied with the bargain he'd made. Rolleen seemed like a pretty levelheaded young woman. They should both be able to accomplish their goals with a minimum of fuss and bother.

"Can I give you a ride home?" he asked.

She started to shake her head, then said, "I suppose

we might as well start getting acquainted. I can show you how to get to my apartment.''

Gavin rolled down his sleeves and buttoned them, then retrieved a navy blue wool sport coat from a hook and slipped it on. He picked up Rolleen's lab coat from the couch and said, ''Have you got a jacket somewhere?''

''In my hospital locker,'' she said.

''Let's go get it.'' He slipped his arm around her waist, and she immediately stiffened.

He kept his arm where it was and looked down at her until she looked back up at him. ''You okay?'' She managed a smile, and he felt her relax slightly.

''I guess this is going to take some getting used to,'' she said. ''Bear with me, will you?''

''Sure.'' He opened the office door and ushered her through it, noticing how soft and feminine her hip felt pressed against his. She was so small tucked in beside him, his protective instincts rose, and he tightened his hold on her waist.

She made a sound of protest in her throat, then made a face and shook her head. ''I'm sorry. It's just... Never mind.''

''What?'' he asked. When she kept her face forward, he said, ''You might as well tell me. We need to learn everything there is to know about each other in the next ten days. As you said yourself, we might as well start now.''

She took a deep breath, let it out and admitted, ''I'm not used to being around men—I mean, this close. I never dated much in high school.'' She shot him a quick, shy smile. ''Too busy being the perfect daughter,'' she explained. ''And I was too busy studying in college so I would be sure to get into medical school. So Jim… He was my first… Jim was my first lover,'' she managed to get out.

Gavin stopped and stared down at her. ''You've got to be kidding.''

''I'm afraid not.''

''So your parents are going to be *shocked* and pleased that you're bringing a man—me—home for Christmas.''

She nodded. ''I never told my family about my relationship with Jim, because he was one of my professors. As far as they're concerned, you'll be the first man I've shown a serious interest in dating.''

''I'm going to get grilled like a hamburger.''

Her gray eyes focused intently on his face. ''I'll let you out of the bargain, if you don't think you can handle it.''

Gavin's lips flattened. Her lack of experience with men might make the situation a bit more difficult, but not impossible. ''I can handle it. I can handle anything.''

Except a four-year-old who isn't your daughter after all.

''Let's get going,'' he said, urging Rolleen down the hall. ''The sooner we get started, the sooner this'll all be over.''

Chapter 2

Rolleen rolled over in bed and groaned. She had invited Gavin Talbot to return to her apartment for lunch at noon today to begin their "courtship."

What was I thinking last night? How could I have agreed to such a bizarre plan? We're never going to get away with it. My family will know right away that we're not really lovers.

Not if she and Gavin Talbot knew everything there was to know about each other. Not if she could successfully pretend she felt affection and admiration for him.

That wasn't going to be too difficult, Rolleen admitted. At least the admiration part. The man was gorgeous. Tall, dark and handsome. The proverbial knight in shining armor riding to the rescue. Intelligent, kind, considerate, compassionate…and sexy.

Yesterday, when Gavin had rubbed her shoulders,

she'd felt the strength of his hands, and the tenderness, and wished she'd tried harder to meet him in August when he'd first called her. She'd been too busy buying books, getting into the routine of classes and catching up with friends she hadn't seen over the summer. Jim Harkness had made his move the first week of classes, and by the time Gavin called the third and fourth times, she was already secretly seeing her professor.

Rolleen swallowed down the acid that rose in the back of her throat. It wasn't the baby making her feel so sick. It was bitterness over Jim's behavior. Just in case, she reached for one of the saltines she kept beside the bed, bit off a corner and began chewing.

She was determined not to let her feelings toward Jim make her ill. Her inexperience with men had led her to misjudge Jim's intentions. She had thought his emotions were as much engaged as hers; he had thought she knew he always had an affair with one of his students. She had been naive. *And in love for the first time.*

Her nose stung and ready tears came to her eyes. Rolleen felt her stomach turn and ran, hand over mouth, for the bathroom. She barely made it in time.

Forget about Jim, she admonished herself a few minutes later, as she rinsed her mouth and pressed a cold, wet washcloth to her face. Rolleen groaned again as she examined herself in the mirror. Her eyes looked less puffy, but they were still bloodshot, and her nose was raw and tender where it had been wiped so many times. She had to stop crying over spilt milk. *Jim's gone from your life forever. You were a fool and an idiot.*

Once. She'd been a fool once. Never again. She would never again give her heart so quickly or completely. Which was why Gavin's offer of a pretend engagement had been so appealing. Her parents would find solace in the fact she was happy and in love with the baby's father, even if she wasn't married. If she went home looking like she looked now, they would feel her pain and suffer along with her.

Rolleen wondered if she would be able to fake with Gavin the same euphoric feelings she'd felt when she'd given herself to Jim—to the man she'd loved—for the first time. Perhaps. But she would have to put a smile on her face to do it. Which meant no more tears.

She dabbed at her eyes with the cool washcloth one more time, then set it aside, looked in the mirror and said, "No looking back, Miss Whitelaw. Think about the wonderful life growing inside you and the joy and happiness ahead of you." That thought brought a smile to Rolleen's face and, amazingly, she felt better.

When Rolleen heard Gavin's knock at the door shortly before noon, she met him wearing a boat-necked, short-sleeved red silk blouse, black designer jeans with a silver-buckled belt, polished-up-but-worn-out black cowboy boots and a practiced smile, looking very much like her old, stylish self.

"Hi, Gavin," she said cheerfully. "Come on in."

He didn't budge. "Rolleen? Is that you?"

She laughed, grabbed his hand and pulled him inside. "Don't tell me I looked so bad last night you don't recognize me."

"You look...different."

"It's the smile," she said, beaming at him. "It was missing last night."

He finally returned her smile with one of his own that nearly took her breath away, revealing a single dimple in his left cheek. "I had no idea you were so beautiful," he said. "It shouldn't be too difficult to convince your folks I fell in love with you."

Rolleen felt something shift inside. The experience was disturbing, because she'd felt something similar the first time she'd laid eyes on Jim. She quelled the feeling. She wasn't interested in getting involved with another man. And unlike Jim, Gavin had made his position clear from the start. This was all *pretend*.

"Come on in and make yourself comfortable," she said, gesturing him inside her one-bedroom apartment. A ceramic, cowboy-dressed Santa, a table-size pine Christmas tree with winking lights and a fragile crystal nativity evidenced her love of everything to do with Christmas.

"Can I get you something to drink?" she asked.

"Nothing right now," Gavin said, searching for a place to sit that wasn't already occupied by something else.

"Let me clear a place for you," she said with a laugh that acknowledged the clutter. "Growing up in a house with so many kids, I always had to put my things away or lose them. Since I've had a place of my own, I guess I've gone a bit overboard in the other direction."

"I never had to be neat, so I'm not," he admitted with a grin that made her heart take an extra thump.

Rolleen quickly turned away from all that powerful sex appeal, moving a stuffed kangaroo she'd bought for the baby the day she'd learned she was pregnant, a book on childbirth and a red-and-green ruffled Christmas pillow from the secondhand sofa to make space for Gavin. "I thought we could talk for a little while before we eat," she said.

By the time she turned around, Gavin had already claimed her favorite overstuffed corduroy chair by shifting copies of *Vogue* and *Elle* and *The New England Journal of Medicine* to the wooden coffee table.

"Are you sure I can't get you something to drink?" she asked, her nerves getting the better of her as she dropped what she'd picked up back onto the couch.

"Nothing for me."

She waffled about where she ought to sit, then settled on the end of the couch closest to him, reminding herself she was a pregnant woman and that letting herself fall for a handsome face was how she'd gotten that way. She pulled off her boots, tucked her red-Christmas-stocking-clad feet under her and leaned on the broad arm, her attention focused on Gavin. She noticed he was sitting on the front edge of the chair, rather than settling into it and looked as uncomfortable as she felt.

"Where should we start?" she asked.

He rose immediately and paced across the sea green carpet, making a detour around her wooden coffee table, which was littered with as many life-style and fashion magazines as medical journals. Rolleen made most of her own clothes and had once upon a time dreamed of becoming a fashion designer—before she realized her parents expected her to pursue one of the professions more commonly chosen by someone of her extraordinary intelligence.

Gavin abruptly stopped pacing and turned to face her, his hands behind his back. "Have you had any second thoughts since last night?"

"Second, third and fourth thoughts," she admitted. "But I haven't changed my mind."

He hesitated, then crossed and settled more comfortably into the chair, this time leaning forward with his forearms braced on his knees. "I've been thinking about it, too. But I couldn't come up with any better plan to solve your dilemma—or mine—so we might as well go for it. What does the J in R.J. stand for?" he asked.

"Jane."

"Rolleen Jane," he said. "I like it."

The hairs stood up on her arms when he said her name. Rolleen rubbed them down and countered, "It's a better name for a doll than a doctor. Rolleen Jane: she speaks, she sits, she wets! R.J. sounds more like somebody you'd want to have deliver your baby."

Gavin chuckled. "How about plain Rolleen."

"*Plain* Rolleen?"

"Make that just Rolleen."

"*Just* Rolleen?"

He laughed and said, "I'm sticking with Rolleen. I like it. By the way, is that what you want to be, an obstetrician?"

"A pediatrician," she corrected.

"Why?"

"Because I love children."

"Then you're glad about the baby?"

She looked down and placed her hand on the gentle

curve where her child was growing inside her, then looked up at Gavin. "I was at first. And I am now."

He nodded with understanding.

She liked that about Gavin, Rolleen decided. He understood so much without her having to explain it. "What kind of doctor are you?" she asked.

He smiled, and the dimple reappeared.

She told herself she wasn't charmed, as he explained, "I'm not a medical student. I'm studying for my Ph.D. in child psychology. Eventually I plan to counsel dying kids."

Rolleen picked a tuft of stuffing from the couch. "To be honest, that sounds like distressing work."

"Difficult," Gavin conceded. "But ultimately quite uplifting." She raised a questioning brow, and he continued, "We're all going to die. Kids with cancer or other debilitating diseases have time to think about it in advance. I help them through denial and bargaining and anger, and from depression to acceptance, before they actually have to face dying."

"I imagine it must be hard to work with someone—to become intimately acquainted with someone—you know is going to die." *Isn't it hard to share their pain?*

She dared a glance at him, looking for an answer to her unasked question, and found it in the eloquent sorrow reflected back to her from his dark eyes.

"They don't all die," he said. "A few of them miraculously recover. I always hope that will happen."

"You're an optimist," she said, suddenly finding it easier to smile. "That's good. My parents would expect me to choose a spouse who believes the glass is half-full, rather than half-empty.''

''Tell me about your life growing up,'' Gavin said. ''The kind of anecdotes you might have shared with me when we were getting to know each other.''

''I've already told you about my nefarious activities in school,'' she said with a smile. ''As far as my family goes…it's been an adventure growing up on a cattle and cutting horse ranch, especially as one of the Whitelaw Brats.''

''Whitelaw Brats?''

She grinned and said, ''Playful pranks and high-spirited, harmless mischief are a time-honored Whitelaw tradition. My brothers and sisters and I—even though all eight of us were adopted—felt compelled to uphold it.''

''For instance?''

''Jewel and I tied a big red bow to the tail of old Mr. Cooper's bull—which wasn't easy, believe me,'' she said, smiling as she remembered how Jewel had held on tight to the bull's tail through the fence while she tied the bow. ''Another time we used a curling iron on Hardy Carmichael's golden retriever, Butch. He was the cutest thing you ever saw when we were done.''

Gavin laughed and said, ''I'm envious. It sounds like you had a lot of fun together.''

Gavin's laughter warmed someplace deep inside Rolleen. The sensation was pleasant, without being threatening, so she didn't fight it.

''It was fun,'' she agreed. ''Especially with so many of us so close to the same age. I'm the eldest at 24, Jewel's 22, Cherry's 21, Avery's 20, Jake's 19,

Frannie's 16, Rabbit's 15—Rabbit's real name is Louis. We call him Rabbit because—''

"He liked vegetables when he was a kid, especially carrots," Gavin finished for her.

She straightened her legs and relaxed into a sprawl on the sofa. "I'm telling you things you already know."

Gavin cleared his throat and said, "I didn't know exactly how old everybody was, although I'd pretty much guessed. By the way, you forgot Colt."

"I saved the best for last," she corrected. "Colt's fourteen and the rebel in the family. He's also the only one of us who was adopted as a newborn, so he's the only one who hasn't known any parents except Zach and Rebecca. All of us kids had a hand in raising him—which is probably why he's such a maverick. Too many cooks spoiling the broth, or something like that."

"I got the impression your father intends for Colt to take over the ranch."

"It wouldn't surprise me if Colt ends up running Hawk's Pride. He's always had an affinity for the land, he rides like he was born on a horse and Dad's been teaching him the business since he was old enough to walk."

"What plans did your parents have for you?" Gavin asked.

"I'm fulfilling them," she said with a smile. The smile faded. "At least I was until..." Rolleen found another imperfection in the secondhand couch and tried to repair it.

"You said last night you plan to leave school and

try to support yourself. What kind of work will you do?''

Rolleen bit her lower lip anxiously. ''I'd rather not say.''

''I need to know everything—all about the real Rolleen Jane Whitelaw—or this isn't going to work,'' Gavin said.

She looked at him and found she couldn't look away. His dark eyes compelled her to share all her secrets. *That's what he does for a living,* a cautionary voice reminded her. *It has nothing to do with you personally.*

''If we start hedging with each other this early in the game, we might as well call it quits,'' he said.

Rolleen lowered her eyes to avoid his scrutiny. Her hands knotted in her lap. Being a sympathetic listener might be his job, but he was good at it, Rolleen conceded. No one knew what she was about to tell Gavin Talbot. Not any of her family, not her friends, not anyone. It had been her deep, dark secret.

She took a deep breath and said, ''There's a salon in Houston called The Elegant Lady that features designer clothing. They've been wanting me to work with them for some time.''

Gavin picked up one of the fashion magazines from the coffee table and thumbed through it. ''What would you do for them?''

''Design clothing.''

Gavin shut the magazine and stared at her. ''Don't you have to go to design school for that? Or have some kind of training and experience?''

Rolleen pulled her knees up to her chest and wrapped her arms around her legs. ''For the past three years I've been selling my designs—that is, fashions I've designed and sewn myself—to The Elegant Lady.''

Gavin's smooth forehead suddenly acquired several deep lines. ''Are you telling me you've been at the top of your class in medical school for the past two years while you've been secretly working as a fashion designer?''

She hugged her knees more tightly, more protectively, to her chest. ''I'll make a good pediatrician.''

''I never said you wouldn't.''

''Designing is a hobby. I do it for fun.''

Gavin eyed her appraisingly. ''It sounds to me like you'd rather be doing it for a living.''

Rolleen stared at Gavin. He was amazingly perceptive. That wasn't so odd, she realized, when you considered what he planned to do with his life. His work depended on reading faces, finding the hidden context in what people said and did. She still found it a bit disconcerting. In the three months she and Jim had been together, her professor had never once intuited that she wasn't perfectly happy in medical school.

''I wouldn't have gone to medical school if I didn't think I would like being a doctor,'' she said.

''But you *love* designing fashions,'' Gavin guessed.

Rolleen sighed, unable to keep the wistfulness from her voice. ''Yes. I do.''

''Can you really make a living at it?''

''Not with as few designs as I've done over the past two years. But yes, with The Elegant Lady committed to buy as much as I can design, I could make a very comfortable living. And I'd be able to work at home, so I could be with the baby.''

"Why didn't you ever tell your parents you'd rather be a fashion designer and just quit medical school?" Gavin asked.

She smiled mischievously. "I'm about to do that, aren't I?"

"But you aren't being honest with them," Gavin said. "They'll think you're giving up something you really want to do because of the baby. If you're so worried about their feelings, why not admit you prefer designing?"

"Because then they'd know I've been lying to them for a very long time," Rolleen admitted.

"I can't imagine Zach and Rebecca not supporting whatever profession you chose. Why lie in the first place?"

"It's hard to explain to someone who's not adopted," Rolleen said.

"Try."

"You have to imagine what it feels like to be abandoned, totally alone in the world, knowing there's no one who really cares if you live or die. Along comes this man and woman who say, 'We'll love you. We'll take care of you. You're precious to us.'" She lifted her eyes and met Gavin's intent, dark-eyed gaze. "You'd want to please those people because they've given you their love. And because if you didn't, they might take it back."

"Zach and Rebecca would never—"

"I know they wouldn't stop loving me," Rolleen interrupted. "That is, intellectually I know it. But inside—" She tapped her heart with a forefinger. "Inside is a frightened six-year-old girl, already forsaken once by parents who said every day they loved her—and then abandoned her one morning at a convenience store.''

Gavin remained silent, giving Rolleen too much time to think...to remember. Her heart was racing, clutching, as it did every time she relived that awful morning.

She had frantically searched the store several times before she got up the courage to approach the clerk and ask, ''Have you seen my mommy and daddy?''

The clerk had taken one look at her, barefoot and dressed in a calico shift with a torn sleeve and the hem half-down and said, ''We don't allow kids in here alone.''

''I came with my mommy and daddy. She's wearing a dress with flowers on it and he's tall and he's got a mustache.''

The clerk had looked out the window for a rundown truck that wasn't there, said a word she knew she wasn't ever supposed to say and then called the police. Rolleen didn't remember much about the rest of what had happened that day. Mercifully she'd been in shock.

As an adult, Rolleen understood that her birth parents had believed they were doing the right thing leaving her to the state welfare system, because she needed clothes and shoes to go to school and food to grow up healthy, and they were too poor to afford them. She still woke up every morning wondering what had happened to them. She still wondered what she could have done differently to keep them from abandoning her.

It had taken a long time to learn to trust again. It had taken a great deal of courage to let herself fall in love. She told herself she had done nothing wrong as a child...or now...except to fall in love with a shallow man. But she had finally learned her lesson. She wasn't going out on that limb again anytime soon.

''Your turn to talk,'' she said to Gavin. ''Why do you need a fiancée over Christmas?''

Gavin had known this moment was coming, and he'd practiced what he was going to say. When he opened his mouth to speak, nothing came out. He shoved both hands agitatedly through his sun-streaked, tobacco-brown hair, then let them fall onto his thighs. He took a deep breath and said, ''My wife died—'' He cut himself off, swallowed hard and corrected, ''— My wife killed herself in January, and this is the first Christmas...'' *That I will spend without her.*

Gavin could not understand the lump in his throat. He shouldn't be missing Susan, shouldn't be feeling pain at the thought of Christmas without her. She had betrayed him. But it wasn't only Susan he was grieving, he conceded, it was what they had been together with Beth—a husband and a wife and child—a loving family.

He shifted his glance to the stuffed kangaroo sitting on the sofa with the tiny baby in her pouch and thought how much Beth would love to have such a toy.

Don't you see? he felt like shouting. *I can't face a little girl I used to love...a little girl who wants me to love her still...when I can't anymore.*

His throat had swollen completely closed, making it impossible to explain anything. His nose stung and his eyes watered and he felt dangerously close to crying.

Telling Rolleen anything about Beth would have to wait. There was plenty of time over the next ten days to tell the whole sordid story. Gavin swallowed back the worst of the misery in his throat and said, "It would be easier if my grandmother and I weren't alone at the ranch over the holidays."

"So I'm going to be a buffer between you and your grandmother?" Rolleen asked.

"Hester and I get along fine," he said brusquely. "It's… She worries about…" He hesitated, then admitted, "I don't want to be alone this Christmas."

Rolleen could only imagine how Gavin felt, losing a wife, but she had lost Jim, and that was close enough to the same thing for her to understand and feel his pain.

Don't feel too much, a voice warned. *Don't get too close.*

Rolleen made herself listen to the voice. If she wasn't careful, she could be hurt again. It was all right to like Gavin Talbot. It was even all right to feel sorry for him. It wasn't all right to get emotionally involved in his life. She had to protect herself. They were two strangers who were going to part company at the end of the holidays. It was not necessary for her to know more than the bare fact that she would be helping him if she came home posing as his fiancée.

"Where's your home?" she asked, tactfully changing the subject.

"The ranch is about an hour south of here."

"That's where we'll be spending Christmas together?"

Gavin's stomach growled loudly.

Rolleen glanced at her watch and realized it was nearly one o'clock. "Lunch!" She bounced up as though one of the ancient couch springs had sprung and said, "You must be starved. Come on into the kitchen. I planned tomato soup and grilled cheese sandwiches. I hope that's all right."

"Sounds great. What can I do to help?"

"You can fix us each a glass of iced tea while I warm up the soup and cook the sandwiches."

During lunch, Gavin kept her riveted—and laughing until her sides were sore—with stories about the kids he was working with at the hospital.

"How can they find so much to laugh about when their lives are so uncertain?" she asked.

"The same way you've been able to laugh today," Gavin said. "Life goes on. You make the best of it. And it beats the heck out of the alternative."

Rolleen started to laugh and yawned instead.

"Looks like you need your beauty rest," Gavin said, standing and collecting the dishes. He was halfway to the kitchen before Rolleen caught up to him with the iced tea glasses. "Thanks," she said. "I guess we're going to have to cut this short. I am feeling a little tired."

"The baby?" he questioned as he settled the dishes in the sink.

She nodded as she put the glasses down on the counter, then placed both hands on her abdomen. "This little darling takes a lot out of me."

"May I?" he asked, gesturing toward her hands.

Rolleen moved her hands aside, and Gavin's hands, large and warm, covered her rounded belly.

"It seems like it ought to be soft, but it's so firm," he said, his hands gently cradling her stomach.

Rolleen felt an ache in her throat. *If only…*

"Don't be sad," he murmured. "I'm here now, baby."

Rolleen started at the use of the endearment. Was it for her? Or was he speaking to the child inside her? The look Gavin directed at her was so concerned, so loving, that she almost believed he really cared. "You called me baby," she pointed out to him.

"I know. We have to practice being in love," he reminded her.

Practice. Pretend. But it felt so *real.* Rolleen couldn't take her eyes off Gavin. His head was lowering toward hers, but she couldn't believe he really meant to kiss her. They'd known each other only a few hours.

He stopped when his mouth was close enough that she could feel his warm, moist breath on her cheek. "May I?"

"Isn't it a little soon to be kissing?" she asked breathlessly.

"We only have ten days to convince some very astute people that we're in love," he said quietly. "That I've had my hands all over you. That I've been inside you."

Rolleen took a hitching breath. "Holy cow."

"Is that a yes?" he said, his lips curling with amusement.

Rolleen nodded and closed her eyes as he pressed

his lips against her own. They were softer than she'd expected and slightly damp.

"You okay, baby?" he murmured.

Her heart pumped a little faster. "Mmm-hmm."

She felt a tingle as his tongue came out to trace her closed lips. "Oh," she whispered in pleasure.

He took advantage of her open mouth to slip his tongue inside, then withdrew before she could protest. He slowly straightened, his gaze focused on hers, so she could see his dark brown eyes were almost black, his lips rigid with desire.

Rolleen felt panicky without knowing why. She put her hand on Gavin's chest to make a space and eased past him. "I think that's enough for today."

He followed her into the living room. "When can you meet with me again?"

"Next week," she said immediately. Rolleen wanted the rest of the weekend to recover from his touch, from the loving addresses, from his surprisingly sensual kiss.

"How about tonight?" he countered.

"So soon?"

"We don't have much time," he reminded her. "And we both have busy schedules during the week. Why don't I take you out for dinner and dancing?"

"Dancing?"

"It'll be fun. Pick you up at eight." He leaned over and gave her a quick kiss on the mouth. "Think of me while you're napping," he whispered in her ear. A moment later he was out the door.

Rolleen felt like she'd been caught up in a tornado that had come and gone and left her not knowing which end was up. When Gavin had tasted her in the kitchen, she'd wanted to keep on kissing him. And just now she'd been thinking how nice it would be if Gavin laid down with her on the bed and held her while she napped.

Snap out of it, R.J.

Rolleen wasn't going to make the same mistake twice. She'd fallen for Jim Harkness in a hurry and look how that had turned out. What she felt for Gavin couldn't be love, but whatever it was, it was dangerous. When he took her dancing tonight—she *loved* dancing—she was going to have to be careful not to like it too much.

Chapter 3

In the ten days since Gavin Talbot had met Rolleen Whitelaw, he had run the gamut of romantic experiences with her. They had gone from a couple just meeting to a couple who had mated—or rather, who could pretend they had. It had been quite an adventure, and Gavin had enjoyed every minute of it. There was only one cloud on his horizon: Rolleen still didn't know about Beth.

He had meant to tell her, but the better he got to know Rolleen, the less willing he was to confess his feelings toward his daughter. Because he was pretty sure when he did, he was going to lose Rolleen's regard. And he wasn't ready for that to happen yet.

Gavin knew he was only postponing the inevitable, but there was always the chance his feelings toward Beth would miraculously change when he saw her again. At least, that was his excuse for keeping Rolleen in the dark about his daughter.

In a matter of hours they would be leaving to spend the holidays with Rolleen's family at her father's ranch in northwest Texas. Gavin couldn't quite believe they were really going through with it.

As he thought back over the previous ten days, Gavin realized that he and Rolleen had become such good friends, it wasn't going to take much acting to pose as someone who loved her. Especially since—if the circumstances hadn't been what they were—they might have become romantically involved.

He would never forget the stunned look in Rolleen's eyes after he'd kissed her that first time. In fact, touching her and tasting her that day at her apartment had been so arousing, he had felt like picking her up and carrying her straight to the bedroom. The hard part had been remembering he didn't have that right, that everything they did was make-believe, because she needed a make-believe father for her unborn child.

It didn't seem fair to let himself start imagining the two of them together. Rolleen had already been hurt by one man who'd loved her and left her. While he might have fallen for her if she'd been free and single, he couldn't very well ignore the fact she was pregnant with another man's child. That complication alone would make any permanent relationship between them difficult, if not impossible.

Yet over the past ten days, Gavin had learned to like Rolleen Whitelaw better than he had liked anyone—man or woman—in his entire life. It was the confounded sexual attraction between them that had him uptight and confused. It wasn't something that had grown gradually. It had been there right from the start.

Rolleen hadn't simply moved to the music that first evening when he had taken her dancing, she had reveled in it. During a slow jazz tune, she had put the back of her hand against his nape, urged his head down and whispered, "I love dancing with you, Gavin. I mean, darling. Darling sounds lovely, doesn't it? Thanks so much for bringing me here tonight, darling."

The mere sound of her voice, that soft, sexy purr, had made his blood roar in his ears. Gavin didn't know when he'd been so aroused by a woman out of bed. His flesh had come alive along every surface where her slim, feminine form molded itself against his, and because it was all supposedly pretend, he had said exactly what he was thinking. "I'm on fire for you, Rolleen."

She made a whimpering sound and shivered and clung even closer to him.

Instinct drove him to lift her so they would fit better, when what he really wanted was to have her prone. He knew it was way too soon for that—or even the pretense of it. Which was when it had dawned on him that nothing was ever going to happen between them, because this was all *pretend*. Even if it felt damned real.

At the end of the evening, he had kissed her chastely on the forehead at her door, refusing her invitation inside for a cup of coffee. He knew better. It was as difficult holding on to his objectivity as it was keeping his distance. But it would have spoiled everything if he'd started kissing her and touching her for real.

The next step in their "courtship" had been an evening of Christmas shopping two days later.

"Shopping?" he'd said, much aggrieved at the idea.

She'd given him a coaxing smile—which had sent his heartbeat up a notch—and said, "Have you done yours?"

He'd been forced to admit, "Not yet."

"Then we might as well do it together. I have lots of people to buy for, and I'm still not done."

She had taken him to a huge mall on the beltway with a parking lot the size of an airport runway. "People actually shop in this madhouse?" he'd asked.

"I come to see all the Christmas decorations," she replied. "And to shop," she conceded with a smile. "I love the excitement and bustle of the crowd and the look of awe and enchantment in the children's eyes when they meet Santa Claus for the first time. And the carolers. I love Christmas music. It's so full of...of joy!"

She had looked up at him, her face as bright and shiny as one of the Christmas balls hanging from the rafters and said, "You may have noticed. I love *everything* about Christmas."

Gavin hadn't recently made a point of admiring the sparkle and glow of Christmas decorations, but he had trouble taking his eyes off of Rolleen's face. He didn't notice the crowds, because he was too busy watching her.

He stopped with her to observe the children being put on Santa's lap to make their Christmas requests—some crying, some laughing, some adorable. Like the shy little girl with short black hair parted in the middle and bangs that fell into her eyes who reminded him of his daughter.

I wonder if Hester has taken Beth to see Santa?

He could easily have slipped Beth into the conversation—if he hadn't felt so guilty at that precise moment. It wasn't Beth's fault Susan had been unfaithful. It wasn't Beth's fault she wasn't his flesh and blood daughter.

Guilt was quickly followed by another, darker emotion. Seeing Beth's face in his mind's eye reminded him that none of her features were his. Thinking of her brought back the anguished feelings of betrayal he had experienced the night he'd read Susan's letter, and it forced him to acknowledge that he was afraid to see Beth this Christmas because his emotions were so close to the surface. He was terrified he might fall to pieces in front of her.

Which was why he found himself Christmas shopping at a mall with Rolleen Whitelaw. She was going to provide the buffer that would allow him to get through this Christmas season with his... He made himself think the words: *my daughter.*

In fact, Rolleen's attitude toward her unborn child, and the fact she was adopted herself, had Gavin reevaluating his behavior toward Beth. If he wanted to keep Rolleen's good opinion—and he did—he needed to treat his daughter in a loving way. But behavior and feelings were two different things. Gavin could change his behavior. He wasn't so sure about his feelings.

"Look, Gavin! Carolers!" Rolleen exclaimed, interrupting his thoughts.

On his own, Gavin wouldn't have paid any attention to the choir in the center of the mall, but he was so fascinated by the radiant look on Rolleen's face that he listened to see what it was she found so inspiring about the music—and was assailed with nostalgic memories.

God rest ye, Merry Gentlemen!
Let nothing you dismay…

Christmas in his home had always been a wonderful blend of the secular and the religious. They had popped popcorn in the fireplace and read Charles Dickens after they opened presents on Christmas Day. His grandmother had kept the traditions alive after his parents died, and Gavin had maintained them with his family.

This year he hadn't been able to think about any of the things that made Christmas a special time of year. That is, until a few days ago. Seeing Christmas through Rolleen's eyes, Gavin wanted to be a part of it again—the gift giving, the music, the decorations…and the spirit of love he seemed to have lost when his wife died.

Gavin vicariously experienced the pleasure Rolleen took in selecting a model airplane for Colt while she explained, "Colt thinks nobody's noticed, but he's crazy about flying."

"Really?" Gavin said. "He never said anything to me about it."

Her lips curved in what was becoming to him an

endearingly familiar smile. "He thinks he's keeping it a secret."

"It's not?"

"Dad gave him a couple of books on the history of flying for his birthday this year, and I've given him a different model airplane every Christmas for the past five. There isn't much you can keep secret in a household as big as ours."

"Yet you think we can manage it?" Gavin asked, dividing the weight of the packages he carried more equally. "Do you really believe we're going to get away without somebody finding out the truth?"

Her smile disappeared for the first time since they'd stepped inside the mall. She settled a package carefully in the crook of his elbow and said, "For everyone's sake, I hope so." She looked up at him and said, "If we were a married couple, and you were madly in love with me, what would you do if I said I was feeling a little tired and needed to sit down?"

Instead of telling her, Gavin acted on impulse. He set all the packages beside a nearby fountain, lifted her into his arms and settled himself on the edge of the fountain with her in his lap. "Are you comfortable now?"

She was too busy laughing to answer him. She had her arms draped around his neck, and as she leaned against him her breasts pillowed against his chest.

"That was wonderful!" she said. "My family will be truly impressed if you make grand gestures like that."

He put his palm against her cheek, angled her face toward his and said, "I didn't do it to impress anybody. I did it for you."

The laughter stopped abruptly and tears misted her eyes. "Oh, Gavin," she whispered. "What a lovely, romantic thing to say. You're so wonderfully convincing. They'll never doubt you are what you say you are."

He tucked her head under his chin, finding it strangely difficult to speak.

Before they left the mall he purchased a selection of eucalyptus-scented bath accessories for his grandmother. Rolleen had been delighted to help evaluate each and every bottle and jar in the store—until the odd mixture of odors had finally made her nauseated.

"Uh-oh," she'd suddenly said, swallowing furiously. "Uh-oh."

"What is it?"

"I think I'm going to be sick."

He'd looked around frantically but there wasn't a bathroom in sight. He urged her out the boutique door, where he remembered seeing a bench in the mall. To his chagrin, the bench was occupied by an elderly couple he wouldn't ordinarily have asked to get up. But he found himself saying to the white-haired woman, "She's pregnant," and looking at the elderly man for understanding.

"Get up, Harold," the woman said, getting up herself, "and let the little lady sit down."

Gavin dropped his load of packages on the floor beside the bench and knelt in front of Rolleen, watching her take deep breaths, praying for the color to come back into her pale, sweat-dotted face as an interested crowd gathered around them.

"She's expecting," the elderly woman informed anyone who would listen.

Gavin knew Rolleen was all right when she suddenly pointed at a little boy across the mall who was squatted down on his heels watching a shark chasing a diver around a bowl of water. She was on her feet and headed for the toy store before he could stop her.

"You take care of her, son," the elderly man said as Gavin grabbed their packages and followed after her. "Nothing is more important than family at Christmas."

The sudden constriction in Gavin's throat had plenty of time to relax while Rolleen bought presents for some kids at the hospital. When she wasn't looking, Gavin purchased a doll for Beth that talked and ate and wet and hid it at the bottom of his single shopping bag. The doll was something Gavin knew Beth wanted, and he realized he was glad to buy it for her, even if she wasn't really his daughter.

He dropped the packages and Rolleen off that night without coming inside. And without mentioning Beth.

Since Rolleen had been the one to select shopping as a joint activity, their next excursion was Gavin's choice. "I vote for a picnic on the beach," he announced.

"It's winter!" she protested.

"This is South Texas. We don't have winter."

"I can't get off during the day."

"We'll go at night."

"All right. I give up," she conceded, throwing up her hands in defeat. "A picnic on the beach. But don't expect me to wear a swimsuit. What can I bring?"

"Yourself. I'll take care of everything else."

The picnic hadn't quite turned out as he'd planned. Gavin had figured they'd drive down to a beach house he owned near Padre Island and make themselves comfortable on the rug in front of the stone fireplace, where he imagined the two of them kissing in the romantic light of a crackling fire.

Unfortunately, when they arrived, the key to the front door proved useless, because the house was sealed with a padlock.

"I knew the caretaker was having trouble with vandals, and I told him to handle it whatever way he thought best," Gavin muttered. "But I had no idea he'd padlock the place."

"Can you get the key from him?"

Gavin shook his head. "He lives in Houston. I usually call before I come down. I'm sorry, Rolleen." He was surprised at how disappointed he felt.

"Why don't we take our picnic down to the beach?" Rolleen suggested.

"It's full of sand crabs and sand fleas and…sand," he said disgustedly.

She laughed. "We'll put down a blanket. Come on!"

She grabbed his hand and headed back to the Jeep to pick up everything they would need. She took off her tennis shoes when they filled with sand and made him take off his Docksiders. Gavin had to admit the sand felt wonderfully cool between his toes, but the salty breeze off the gulf was downright chilly.

"You're going to catch a cold," he protested when she shivered despite the sweatshirt she was wearing over a pair of faded cutoffs. "This was a mistake."

"It was a fabulous idea," she countered, her arms spread wide, her head back as she turned circles staring up at the night sky. "I've never been to the beach before."

He hurried to keep up with her as she skipped over a sand dune and down onto the beach. "Never?"

She shook her head, her windblown hair catching in her mouth. "Not a lot of ocean in northwest Texas. And I've been too busy with school to get down here."

Rolleen had trouble spreading the blanket by herself with all the wind, and Gavin had to drop what he was carrying and help her. They put picnic items on the four corners of the blanket to keep it from flying. Rolleen finally settled onto the blanket cross-legged and grabbed his hand to pull him down beside her.

Gavin laughed as he settled on the center of the blanket. "The picnic basket's holding down the north corner of the blanket. We're going to starve unless we sit closer to it."

"Not yet," she said, squeezing his hand.

When he looked into her gleaming eyes she said, "Couldn't we just lie back and look at the stars for a little while?"

She held on to his hand as she lay back on the blanket, and Gavin laid himself down beside her. They said nothing for a very long time. Gavin looked at the stars and found the Big Dipper and the North Star, which was the extent of his knowledge of astronomy.

He was very much aware of the fact Rolleen was flat on her back and how little effort it would take to pull her into his arms. He kept waiting for her to make some overt move toward him, to give him some signal that she wanted to do more than hold hands. But it didn't come.

"Pretty moon," he said at last.

"Yes, it is."

"Not a cloud in the sky."

"No," she said softly. "Just billions of stars. Do you suppose the star that led everyone to Bethlehem is still up there somewhere?"

"I don't know why not," he said. "You see a particular star you think might be it?" he asked, glancing at her.

"The brightest one."

He searched the sky, but they all looked about the same to him. He made himself see the sky through Rolleen's eyes and found one faraway star that winked brighter than the rest. "I see it," he said.

She squeezed his hand again, and he felt connected to her and in some odd way to the sand and the sea and the sky as well.

"Rolleen?" He heard the yearning in his voice but by then was beyond feeling pride. He wanted to hold her. He wanted to touch her. "We've been seeing each other for a week."

He saw her swallow hard. "I know. A wonderful week."

He opened his mouth to suggest they should graduate from holding hands, maybe indulge in another kiss, but bit his tongue before he spoke. She was right. It had been a wonderful week without the kissing and touching. He didn't need to indulge in the acts to know he wanted her, to *pretend* for her parents' sake that he wanted her.

To his surprise, she rolled onto her side facing him. "Gavin, would you kiss me, please?"

He soughed out a breath he hadn't known he'd been holding, then rolled onto his side facing her. There wasn't much space between them, just enough so he didn't have to look cross-eyed at her. "I'd like very much to kiss you, Rolleen," he said. "That's why I'm not so sure it's such a good idea."

She thought about that a minute and said, "Neither of us wants this charade to lead to entanglements. But I think we'd better do this anyway."

"Why?"

"Because my sister Jewel is going to ask me when I knew I was in love with you, how it felt, what we did. And I want this to be that moment. I think you should kiss me, so I'll have a lovely memory I can share with her."

Gavin's heart was in his throat, making it impossible to speak. He eased Rolleen onto her back and shifted his body over hers, holding his weight on his elbows, settling his body into the warm, welcoming cradle of her thighs. "All right, Rolleen," he said quietly. "Let's make a memory together."

He threaded his hands into her hair and angled her beautiful, vulnerable face up to his in the moonlight before he lowered his mouth and touched his lips to hers.

"Gavin."

The reverent sound of his name on her lips made his chest ache. He wanted to be gentle, to be tender, to be soft and giving and all the things a woman wanted from a man at such a moment. But he found himself plundering her mouth, grasping her hair to keep her from escaping his rough, urgent kisses, desperately taking what he wanted, what he needed from her. His tongue broached her lips, mimicking the sex act, as he pressed his body against hers, claiming her, making her his—if only for this brief moment.

She was a willing captive. Her arms came around his shoulders and held him tight, her fingernails digging into his skin through his sweatshirt as her body arched up beneath him. Her tongue thrust into his mouth, surprising him and inflaming him. He became a feral animal, without thought or conscience, wanting only one thing.

Gavin suddenly made a sound like a cat caught in a ringer and came up off of Rolleen like he'd been popped from a toaster. "Yow!" he yelled, jackknifing and grabbing for his toe.

"What is it?" Rolleen cried.

"A crab bit my toe!"

Rolleen giggled.

Gavin got the crab off a second before Rolleen shrieked and flapped her hands and cried, "There's a crab in my *hair!*"

Gavin laughed and scooted over to help her. "Be still so I can find it!" he said, gripping both her trembling hands in one of his. He pulled the crab free with the other and threw it aside, then stood and helped her up. "I guess we'd better find another picnic spot." And then, "I'm sorry about that memory you wanted to make."

"Don't be!" she said with a soft laugh. "This was absolutely perfect. Especially the part where the crab bit your toe."

"What?"

"Don't you see? It's so *real*. Who could make up a story like that?"

Gavin chuckled. "I see what you mean."

Rolleen leaned over and opened the picnic basket. "What have you got in here that I could nibble on? I'm starving!"

Gavin gave her a fried chicken leg and helped himself to a couple of deviled eggs, while they stood in the center of the blanket watching for crabs. When they'd demolished the contents of the picnic basket, Gavin put his Docksiders back on and started putting things away. "I think we'd better get started back."

Rolleen yawned as she tied her tennis shoe. "I'm afraid I won't be much company during the ride back. I'm pretty worn out."

"The baby," they said together. They shared a look that made Gavin feel they had shared a whole lot more. He forced his gaze away and said, "We'd better get going."

"Thank you, Gavin," she said. "I had a lovely time."

"No thanks necessary," he replied.

Five minutes after they were on the road in his Jeep, she was sound asleep, her head nestled against his shoulder, her hand resting on his thigh. Gavin felt protective and possessive—both appropriate emotions for a prospective groom. Which he was...and he wasn't.

There had been other enjoyable evenings together in the last few days of their "courtship"—studying together in the library, playing billiards in a yuppie game room, doing laundry, going through each other's medicine cabinets and kitchens, sitting down with Rolleen's photo albums and discussing all the intimate details of each other's friends and family.

Except for Beth. Somehow the subject of Beth just never came up.

Gavin had let himself fall in love with Rolleen. He figured it was silly to fight his feelings for her, at least until the game was played out with her family and with his. Until then, the more in love with her he could pretend to be, the better. But it was beginning to feel more real…and less pretend.

"Gavin? Are you all right?"

Gavin realized he must have been daydreaming for quite some time. "I'm fine, Rolleen. Are you all packed?"

She set down a small suitcase next to the shopping bags full of gifts she was taking home. "I think I have everything." She rubbed her hands together nervously as she looked around her living room.

He caught her hands between his and said, "Don't worry so much, sweetheart. Everything will be fine."

She tried for a smile but couldn't quite make it. "I'm not even used to having you call me sweetheart."

Gavin put his arms around her and rocked her back and forth in a comforting hug. He kissed her forehead and her cheeks and her nose and finally planted a quick kiss on her mouth. "Just don't forget I love you."

She looked up into his eyes and said, "And I love you."

Gavin caught his breath as she rose on her tiptoes and kissed him softly on the mouth. She teased his lips until he opened for her and her tongue slid into his mouth, giving him a brief taste of her, before she ended the kiss.

"Breathe," she whispered, the familiar mischievous smile on her face.

Gavin gasped a breath of air, tucked her head under his chin and held her tight against his thudding heart.

Don't forget she's playing a role.

"One more thing before we go," he said, pushing her away. He reached into the sport coat he was wearing with a button-down shirt and jeans and retrieved a small black box. He opened it and held it out to her. "This is for you."

She gasped and her eyes went wide as she retrieved the one-carat marquise diamond engagement ring from its velvet bed. "It's exquisite," she said as she slipped it on.

"I hope it fits all right."

"It's perfect. In every way." She met his gaze and said, "Thank you, Gavin. Are you sure you'll be able to return it later?"

"It belonged to my mother," he said.

"Oh."

She started to pull it off, but he stopped her. "I'd like you to wear it. Susan didn't— Susan never— It hasn't been worn since my mother died."

Her eyes brimmed with tears, and she put her arms around his neck and hugged him tight. "It's beautiful, Gavin," she said, her voice ragged. "Thank you."

Gavin pulled her arms away, cleared his throat and said, "We'd better get moving. We don't want to keep your family waiting."

Chapter 4

"It's good to be home," Rolleen said as Gavin drove their rental car under a black wrought-iron archway that spelled out HAWK'S PRIDE.

Hawk's Pride had originally been a part of her grandfather's ranch, Hawk's Way, which had been settled by Whitelaws more than a century before. The grassy plains stretched for miles, and the steep canyon walls were etched with primitive drawings left by those who had roamed the land before the white man had come to settle it. The several-thousand-acre parcel her father owned had been given to him on his twenty-first birthday to do with as he liked.

Zach Whitelaw had built a whitewashed, Spanish-style adobe ranch house in a square around an enormous, moss-laden live oak, creating a lovely central courtyard where Rolleen had spent hours in her youth dreaming up exotic fashions. She loved her home every bit as much for its rich heritage as she did for its majestic beauty.

"The house is lit up like a Christmas tree," Gavin said. "I guess they waited up for us."

"I told you they would." Although Rolleen almost wished they hadn't. She and Gavin had made the trip to northwest Texas in his private plane, so there hadn't been any flight connections to tire her out, but worry about what her family would say when they saw Gavin and found out she was pregnant had taken its toll.

She directed Gavin around to the kitchen door, since only strangers used the front entrance. When she and Gavin stepped inside, Rolleen found her family gathered around the central island in the kitchen drinking egg nog and eating Christmas ribbon cookies.

"Rolleen!" sixteen-year-old Frannie shrieked. "You're home!"

"Welcome home, honey," her mother said with a smile and a hug.

"Rolleen's home!" her brother Jake announced to anyone who was listening.

The cacophony of greetings was deafening, and Rolleen did her part to make a joyful noise. Still bundled up against the cold, her nose a frozen berry, she was hugged and kissed and kissed and hugged as she was passed from one family member to another.

"You remember Gavin," she said to her mother and father, staying close to Gavin with an effort as their coats and scarves were taken away by Avery and Jake and the shopping bags full of gifts were taken to be put under the tree by Colt and her sister Jewel's fiancé, Mac Macready.

Rolleen waited for someone to notice her bulging stomach beneath her waistless dark green velveteen dress, but they were all distracted by Gavin's presence. "I invited Gavin to spend Christmas with us." She held out her hand, displaying the ring, and said, "We're engaged."

"Wow!" Frannie said, grabbing her hand. "Look at the size of that diamond!"

"You're drooling, Frannie," her twenty-year-old brother Avery said, using a forefinger to tip her gaping mouth closed. "Welcome to the family," he added, shaking Gavin's hand.

"You play football?" nineteen-year-old Jake asked as he shook Gavin's hand, a football curved under his opposite arm.

"A little," Gavin said, surprising Rolleen, who had never thought to ask.

Jewel gave Gavin a hug and said, "What a marvelous surprise! I'm so glad for you both."

Mac buffeted Gavin on the shoulder, smiled shrewdly and said, "Congratulations."

"Hi there, Gavin. Nice to see you again," Colt said, gripping Gavin's hand and pumping it up and down. "I can hardly believe you're going to be my brother-in-law after all," he said with a wink.

Gavin laughed, squeezed Rolleen's waist and said, "I just had to find the right Whitelaw woman."

"What's that mean?" Frannie asked.

Colt proceeded to tell the whole family his version of one of the many stories Gavin had told Rolleen. How Gavin had been attracted to Jewel when he first met her at the beginning of his summer at Camp LittleHawk and how Mac Macready, who'd been at Hawk's Pride recovering from a pro football injury, had quickly staked his claim on Jewel, cutting him out.

"Mac just flat outmaneuvered you," Colt said with a laugh.

Rolleen shot a worried glance at Gavin, who seemed to be taking her family's jests with good humor. She had never considered how overwhelming a Whitelaw welcome might seem to him, compared with his smaller family gatherings. Her eyes never left his face as her family escorted them like a circus parade from the kitchen to the living room.

"It's good to see you again, Gavin," her father said as soon as Rolleen and Gavin were seated side by side on the worn saddle-brown leather couch. "I have to admit I'm curious, though. How did you and Rolleen meet?"

Rolleen exchanged an amused look with Gavin. He checked his watch, reached for his wallet and handed her a five-dollar bill.

"What was that all about?" her mother asked.

"I made a bet with Gavin that Daddy would start asking questions within sixty seconds after he sat down," Rolleen replied with a grin.

"So how long have you two known each other?" her mother asked.

Rolleen looked at her watch, held out her hand again and Gavin put another five dollars in it.

Her mother laughed. "Anyone else you'd like to have ask a question?" she asked Rolleen.

"Nope. I only bet on sure things." She wasn't willing to hazard a guess at what might transpire over the course of the next few days. She had her fingers crossed for luck, because she was going to need it.

Her entire family—except Cherry and her husband Billy, who were at the Stonecreek Ranch putting their three children to bed—arranged themselves around her and Gavin in the living room. Her mother had settled in the pine rocker by the warmth of the crackling fire in the stone fireplace. Her father stood right behind her mother, his hands resting on her shoulders.

Mac Macready sat in a brass-studded, wine-colored leather chair, with Jewel angled crosswise on his lap. Her brothers and sisters had found comfortable spots on the Navajo rug, leaning against each other and the furniture. Despite the fact there was room, no one joined them on the couch.

Someone was crooning, "Chestnuts roasting on an open fire," on the CD-player, and the house smelled of the pine boughs decorating the mantel. Rolleen took a deep breath and let it out. She was home.

Her gaze lingered on the ten-foot-tall spruce hung with all the homemade Santas and reindeer and angels that all of them had created in six years of elementary school. Festive colored lights winked from behind store-bought ornaments that had been selected, one by each child in the family, every Christmas since Jewel had been adopted seventeen years ago. Rolleen located the glittery star, lace angel and graceful, feathery swan that were among her favorites.

"To answer your question, Mr. and Mrs. Whitelaw—" Gavin began.

"You called me Zach last summer," her father reminded him.

Gavin cleared his throat. "I wasn't sure whether…I mean—"

"You're Rolleen's fiancé and our guest," her mother said with a welcoming smile. "Make yourself at home. And don't you dare call me Mrs. White-law."

Gavin laughed, and Rolleen felt her heart swell with emotion. He was so good to be helping her this way. And she could have kissed her parents for making him so welcome.

"To answer your question," Gavin said to her father, "Rolleen and I have known each other since August, when I followed up on Jewel's suggestion that I call and introduce myself to her when I returned to Houston." Gavin gave Rolleen a look that made her toes curl and added, "It was the most important call I've ever made."

Rolleen heard the silence after Gavin's pronouncement and felt the blood creeping up her throat. Gavin didn't have to lay it on quite so thick, did he? She glanced up at him and completely lost her train of thought. He was looking at her like a man besotted, like he wanted to hold her forever, like he loved her with all his heart. When Zach cleared his throat, it broke the spell and Rolleen turned to her father, aware of the twin spots of heat on her cheeks that declared her guilty conscience…and her involuntary physical response to Gavin's intense, loving gaze.

"We…uh…we kind of hit it off," she said lamely.

"I guess so!" Avery said with a snicker.

"Avery," her mother reproved.

"When are you two getting married?" Frannie asked.

"He just got here, Frannie," Rabbit said, nudging her in the ribs. "Give him a chance to breathe."

Frannie glared at Rabbit, then turned to Rolleen and said, "Well, when?"

Rolleen watched in awe—along with her family—as Gavin lifted her palm to his lips and kissed it.

"We haven't set a date yet," he said, smiling into Rolleen's eyes.

Rolleen dared a glance around the room and saw that as far as her family was concerned, the deed was as good as done. She wondered if Gavin knew what he'd let himself in for. Now that he was nearly one of the family, he could expect to be treated like one of the family, which meant no question was too personal, no inquiry off-limits.

Without warning, Rolleen's stomach churned, and she tasted acid at the back of her throat. Oh, no. She couldn't be sick now! Morning sickness was supposed to come in the morning. She wanted time to let her parents see her and Gavin together before they discovered she was pregnant. She wanted time— But there wasn't time.

Rolleen shot a desperate look at Gavin, who had been through enough moments like this over the past ten days to recognize the problem. She needed a bathroom in a hurry. But how could they manage it and still keep her secret?

To her surprise, Gavin didn't even try. He rose, bringing Rolleen to her feet at the same time, and said, "You'll have to excuse Rolleen. She needs a bathroom. Now."

Her family stared at her bemused for perhaps two

seconds before Jewel grabbed her hand and pulled her toward the bathroom down the hall. Rolleen stared helplessly over her shoulder at Gavin, who was left standing in the middle of her gape-mouthed family.

Rolleen didn't have much time to worry about Gavin's upcoming interrogation before she was leaning over the toilet bowl with Jewel's gentle hand on her shoulder. Jewel handed her a damp cloth to wipe her mouth, flushed and put the seat down so Rolleen could sit on it.

Jewel settled on the edge of the tub, her knee nearly touching Rolleen's, and said, "When's the baby due?"

"You haven't even asked if I'm pregnant!" Rolleen said.

"Is it food poisoning? Stomach flu? Indigestion?" Jewel shot back.

"No."

"When?" Jewel repeated.

"The end of May."

Jewel's lips curled in amusement. "It must have been love at first sight. You just met Gavin in August."

"We...we..."

"I can see he loves you," Jewel said. "Do you love him?"

"I...uh..."

Jewel put a hand on Rolleen's knee. "You do love him, don't you?"

Rolleen looked into Jewel's ordinary brown eyes and saw a wealth of compassion and caring. Tears sprang to Rolleen's eyes, and she tried to blink them away.

"Oh, Rolleen," Jewel said, going to her knees on the bath mat and taking Rolleen's hands in her own. "I feel like this is all my fault, since I was the one—"

"I *do* love him," Rolleen sobbed. "He's the most wonderful man in the world!"

"Then what's wrong?" Jewel asked, perplexed.

"I… He… We…" Rolleen was on the verge of blurting the truth, when she caught herself. Their charade had a purpose, which was preserving Christmas for her family. If she told Jewel the truth, she knew that before the holiday was over she'd end up telling everyone. As bad as lying made her feel, she was certain telling the truth would be infinitely worse.

What had made her cry was the realization that she was beginning to have dangerously loverlike feelings for Gavin Talbot. He was a wonderful man, and he'd played the role of doting husband-to-be to perfection. What frightened her was the strength of her feelings for him on such short acquaintance. She refused to become a victim of the same sort of infatuation she'd had for her professor. She was desperately fighting the feelings she had for Gavin that felt like love and miserable because of it.

She swallowed back the acid in her throat and said, "Gavin wanted to marry me right away, but I thought it would be better to wait and make sure we're right for each other first. I'm so confused. I don't know what to do."

"You always did think too much," Jewel chided. "What about the baby?" she asked. "Is Gavin happy about the baby?"

Rolleen realized she and Gavin had never discussed the baby. She'd avoided the subject, knowing it wasn't going to be Gavin's concern. But she needed an answer for her sister. "Gavin seems fascinated by the whole process," she extemporized, remembering how he had marveled at the firm roundness of her body where the baby was growing inside her.

"That's a good sign," Jewel said. "So tell me. When did you know you were in love?"

Rolleen smiled, relieved that she had a story to tell that would ring true. "We were at the beach," she began, "having a picnic."

"How romantic! I don't think I should be the only one to hear this," Jewel said. "Otherwise, you're just going to have to tell it again for everybody else. Do you feel well enough to rejoin the family?"

Rolleen nodded, and the two of them left the bathroom. Even from down the hall, she could hear Gavin discussing her pregnancy. She hurried toward the living room, wondering what he'd been asked and what, exactly, he'd told her family.

The moment Rolleen was gone from the room, Gavin had taken one look at her family's faces and known he was in trouble. "Rolleen's pregnant," he announced baldly. "She's still having a little morning sickness." He settled back onto the couch, crossed his ankle over his knee and pretended to be comfortable while he waited for the inquisition to begin.

"Why aren't you married?" Zach asked.

Gavin wasn't fooled by the calm voice. Zach's body was one giant knot of tension, and a muscle jerked in his cheek where he had his teeth clenched. His eyes bored into Gavin's, demanding an answer…the right answer.

Gavin and Rolleen had discussed in some depth exactly what to say to relieve her parents' concern. He gave the prepared response. "Rolleen decided she'd like a little more time to make sure we're right for each other before we marry."

"It's a little late for that, don't you think?" Zach said in a hard voice. "With a baby on the way?"

Gavin's foot came down, and he sat forward, his arms braced on his knees, his body taut in a visceral response to the threat Zach posed. "I wouldn't force any woman into a marriage she didn't want."

"You should have thought of that before—"

Rebecca put a hand on Zach's arm to cut him off. "We can see you love her," she said.

Gavin opened his mouth to confirm it and couldn't get the words out. He hated lying to these people. He looked around and saw frowns and confusion where a few moments before there had been smiles and realized that the lies were a temporary, necessary solution to a very difficult situation. "I assure you—all of you—that I have every intention of making sure Rolleen's taken care of in the future."

That was no lie. He liked Rolleen well enough to keep an eye out for her when this was all over. There were a few advantages to being filthy rich. He'd make certain Rolleen had whatever she needed to keep her and the baby comfortable until she was earning enough designing fashions to manage on her own.

Gavin heard an audible sigh of relief in the room, and the expressions of concern eased into curiosity.

"What about medical school?" Colt asked. "Is Rolleen going to be able to finish?"

"You'll have to ask Rolleen about that," Gavin hedged.

"I'm planning to quit," Rolleen announced as she stepped from the hall into the living room. "So I'll have more time for the baby."

Gavin rose and reached out a hand to Rolleen, who took it and let him reseat her on the couch beside him. He put a protective arm around her shoulder, knowing what was probably coming. This was the point at which Rolleen expected the most resistance from her parents.

He had argued she ought to tell them the truth—that she planned to replace medical school with designing fashions. She had pointed out that her parents would be more suspicious of her starting a brand-new career with a brand-new baby, than with the notion of her quitting medical school and being supported by her husband.

From the corner of his eye Gavin saw she was right. The look her parents exchanged was pure anxiety.

"If it's a matter of money—" Zach began.

"It isn't," Rolleen interrupted. "It's a choice I've made freely."

Gavin watched Zach's lips flatten, saw Rebecca's mouth purse. He could see what they were thinking. *How freely could the decision be made when Rolleen so obviously hadn't planned to become pregnant?* Which made him the villain. The accusation *Why weren't you more careful?* was plain on her father's face. And her mother's eyes clearly revealed her regret that things hadn't turned out more perfectly for her daughter.

Rolleen miscalculated, Gavin thought. It wasn't enough to have the father of her child on hand. Her parents weren't going to be happy until the two of them were tied up good and proper. Gavin shoved a restless hand through his hair. He'd gone as far as he was willing. Her family would have to make the best of the situation, and if it spoiled Christmas for them...

He felt Rolleen's hand on his thigh and looked at her in surprise at the intimate touch. Her gaze was focused on her father as she said in a quiet, intense voice, "I love him, Daddy." She turned to her mother and said, "Please, Mom, I love him."

Gavin turned to see whether her declaration had made a difference, and realized he had underestimated Rolleen's understanding of her parents. He watched the tension ease out of her father's shoulders and saw the loving smile appear on her mother's face. Those few words had turned the tide.

"Welcome to the family, Gavin," Zach said.

Gavin was amazed and relieved at how quickly their charade had been accepted.

"Now, Rolleen," Jewel said, "tell us when and how you fell in love with Gavin."

Gavin couldn't believe how personal the question was, or that Jewel expected Rolleen to relate something so private in front of her entire family. But they all waited with bated breath, their bodies angled forward expectantly, their eyes focused on Rolleen.

He felt Rolleen's hand caress his thigh and realized his body was reacting involuntarily to her touch. He flushed and grabbed her hand, holding it in his. She looked up at him, then smiled mischievously when she realized the problem.

"Why don't you tell them when you first fell in love with me, Gavin?" she teased.

Gavin was flustered. He knew the story on the beach belonged to her. That was the moment *she* had fallen in love with *him*. But they'd never come up with a moment when he'd first known he was in love with her. Gavin felt the tension mount as her family waited for him to speak.

When did I fall in love with her? When did I know she was someone special? When could I have given her my heart?

He looked into Rolleen's soft gray eyes and feelings he had kept hidden deep inside came pouring out. "From the first moment I laid eyes on Rolleen—late one night at the hospital—I wanted to hold her in my arms. And when we kissed for the first time, I knew my life would never be the same." Saying the words, Gavin felt drawn to Rolleen, connected to her, and he obeyed the urge to lean down and touch her lips with his.

He had forgotten entirely about her family, about where they were, about pretense. His mouth molded itself to hers, and he tasted her sweetness, her gentleness.

"Hey, you two. Break it up!" Jewel said with a laugh. "I want to hear how Rolleen fell in love with you!"

Gavin looked up to find Rolleen's family smiling—grinning was more like it—at the two of them. Well, he'd done his part. They were convinced the romance was real. He leaned back on the couch, keeping Rolleen close with his arm around her shoulder and said, "Your turn, sweetheart."

He saw the panicked look in her eyes and whispered to her, "You can do it. I'm here if you need me."

"No secrets!" Rabbit said. "We want to hear everything!"

"I was just advising your sister to edit the story for innocent ears," Gavin said.

"Oh, yeah," Rabbit said, blushing to the roots of his hair.

"Tell us everything!" Frannie urged.

"The truth is, I fell in love with Gavin at the beach," Rolleen began.

Gavin listened to her story with as much rapt attention as her family. For the first time, he was hearing what she'd been feeling that night, or rather, the story she'd made up about what she'd been feeling that night.

She turned and looked deep into his eyes. "It's hard to describe the mood I was in exactly." She broke away and said, "But imagine the moon and a million stars overhead—one star a little brighter than all the others—and the smell of the sea and the sound of the waves crashing on the shore and..." She focused her gaze on him again. "And a pair of beautiful, dark brown eyes staring down at me with such love... How could I not love him back?"

"What happened then?" Frannie asked.

Jake elbowed her and said, "Can't you guess?"

"Did he kiss you?" Frannie guessed.

Rolleen turned to them, smiled and said, "Yes. And then—"

"Rolleen—" her mother warned.

"A crab bit Gavin's toe!"

The whole family broke into raucous laughter. Gavin pulled Rolleen close and gave her a quick kiss on the nose to reward her for getting through the story and ending it on just the right note. At that moment she yawned hugely and they both said "The baby!" and everyone laughed again.

"You need your rest," her mother said, coming forward to grab Rolleen's hand and pull her onto her feet. "Let's get you settled. We can all talk more in the morning."

While Gavin watched, Rolleen left the room with her mother, followed by Jewel and Frannie close on their heels.

Mac stretched and said, "Guess I'll be heading over to the counselor's cottage. I expect Jewel will be here a while yet. Tell her I'll wait up for her, will you, Zach?"

"Sure," Zach said. "Now, Gavin, where shall we put you?"

"I'd be glad to stay in the counselor's cottage where I spent the summer," Gavin said.

Zach shook his head. "We're remodeling, so the heat's off. I wouldn't feel comfortable having Rolleen stay out there."

Gavin worked hard not keep his mouth from gaping. Zach planned for him and Rolleen to spend the night together? When they weren't married? Rolleen had assured him her parents would separate them. He couldn't very well ask to be put in a different room from "the woman he loved" without arousing suspicion. But this was going to cause some problems he and Rolleen hadn't discussed.

Rebecca reappeared in the living room with Fran-

nie and Jewel and said, ''Jewel's volunteered to let
Frannie stay in the second bedroom at the cottage, so
Gavin and Rolleen can share Rolleen's old bed-
room.''

''Good. That's settled,'' Zach said. ''We'd all better hit the sack. We have a lot of things planned for
tomorrow.''

Zach slapped Gavin on the back as he passed by,
and Avery, Jake, Rabbit and Colt each said good
night and headed down the two halls to their rooms.
Jewel gave Gavin a quick hug before she ushered
Frannie toward the kitchen door.

''Rolleen's room is on the back side of the
square,'' Rebecca said. ''Go down the hall, make a
right hand turn, then make another right hand turn.''

''I'll come by later and make sure you have everything you need and say good night to Rolleen,'' Zach
said.

''Fine,'' Gavin said. But he avoided looking into
Zach's eyes as he headed for Rolleen's bedroom.

Chapter 5

Rolleen's first inkling that her parents planned to put Gavin in her bedroom occurred when Colt knocked at her door and set Gavin's suitcase next to hers.

"Mom said I should bring this in here."

"What?"

Colt hesitated. "Would you rather Gavin stayed somewhere else? I can tell Mom—"

"No," she interrupted, recovering her composure. "Of course I want him to stay with me," she fibbed. "I just never expected Mom and Dad—"

"To put you two in the same room when you aren't married yet," Colt finished for her.

She nodded.

"They already went through this once with Jewel and Mac," Colt explained, setting down the suitcase. "Dad told me the important thing was they loved each other, and they were committed to each other. I guess he figures that's true of you and Gavin, too. Especially with a baby on the way.''

''Of course,'' Rolleen whispered, because that was all the sound she could get past the knot of guilt in her throat. ''Thanks, Colt. I'll see you in the morning.''

Colt looked like he wanted to say more, but Rolleen already had her hand on the door to close it behind him. She hurried to get her clothes changed before Gavin showed up. She had taken her dress off but hadn't yet found her pajamas in her suitcase when she heard a soft knock at the door.

''It's me,'' Gavin said. ''Let me in.''

''Just a minute.'' She threw things out of her suitcase, hunting desperately for the black silk Chinese pajama set she had brought.

''I'm coming in, Rolleen. Otherwise somebody's going to catch me lurking in the hall and start asking questions.''

''Gavin, don't—'' She found the pajamas at the same instant she heard him open and shut the door. She whirled to face him in her plain white underwear and bra, holding the wadded up silk pajamas in front of her. ''I'm sorry about this,'' she said. ''I had no idea they'd put us together.''

She felt flustered standing before Gavin in the bedroom she'd shared with Jewel growing up. Especially with him staring at her as though he'd never seen a half-dressed woman. ''Would you mind turning around so I can finish getting changed?''

He cleared his throat, said ''Sure'' and turned his back. ''I'll sleep on the floor,'' he volunteered.

''There's plenty of room for both of us on the bed.''

She watched him turn to eye the brass-railed double bed over his shoulder and realized he'd also caught a glimpse of her bra coming off.

He quickly turned away, cleared his throat again and said, ''I don't think it would be a good idea for us to sleep in the same bed.''

''We're both grown-ups,'' Rolleen said, feeling more comfortable in the concealing black silk pajamas, which covered her from throat to ankle. She stuffed her bra and panties into her suitcase and slid it to the floor. ''You can turn around now.''

He turned slowly, his eyes lowered.

Rolleen had never felt more like a grown-up than she did as Gavin's gaze moved from her bare toes up her legs to her silk pajama shirt, which was slit up the front so that flesh showed at her midriff. She felt her nipples peak even before his gaze got to her breasts and quickly crossed her arms to hide her unexpected—and unwanted—reaction. His gaze caught at the Chinese-style frog closure at her throat, and she was breathing like she'd done a hundred sit-ups by the time his eyes finally met hers.

''That's some outfit,'' he said. ''Did you design it?''

She nodded jerkily.

He took a step toward her, and she resisted the impulse to retreat.

He paused and said, ''I just want to feel the material, if that's all right.''

''Oh. Go ahead.''

He took two more steps and reached out to caress

the soft fabric at her waist. "I'd like to be these pajamas right now," he murmured.

Rolleen was entranced by the ardent look in his eyes, by the raspy sound of his voice. He began gathering the silk fabric in his hand, exposing more of her midriff and at the same time pulling her closer, erasing the distance between them. "Gavin…"

She could have stopped him at any time. He hadn't laid a hand on her—only the silk. She let him draw her near enough that she could see he had ridiculously long eyelashes for a man, close enough that his intent, dark brown eyes made her think of hot, melted chocolate. "Gavin, we shouldn't—"

His lips touched hers, and she felt her knees buckle. She made a helpless sound in her throat and felt his arm slide around her waist to pull her tight against him and hold her upright. He explored her lips with his, tasting, touching, testing.

Soft. So very soft. And gentle. And teasing, she thought.

He made her want. He made her yearn. He made her regret.

Rolleen turned her face away and pressed her cheek hard against Gavin's chest, hoping he wouldn't notice how much she was trembling. "There's no one here to see us now," she reminded him.

"Your father said he'd be by to say good night," he said in a husky voice. "I thought you ought to look kissed."

"Oh."

She instinctively jerked her head away when the knock came on the door, but Gavin's hand around her waist kept her close to him.

"Come in," he said.

Rolleen expected to feel embarrassed when her father found her in Gavin's arms. But the look of relief on her father's face when he realized Gavin was making love to her made her grateful to him for being so perceptive. "Did you want something, Daddy?" she asked.

"Only to make sure you both have everything you need."

She felt Gavin's eyes on her and his grating reply, "I've got everything I could ever want or need right here in my arms."

Her father looked pleased, and she was sorry this was only an act. She made herself smile and say, "Good night, Daddy."

"Good night, honey. See you both at breakfast," he said as he pulled the door closed behind him.

Rolleen hid her face against Gavin's chest, feeling the awful weight of her deception.

"I know that was tough," he said. "But think of the alternative."

"Thank you, Gavin," she said, enjoying the way his hand smoothed over her hair.

"For what?"

"For doing this for me. For pretending—"

He kissed her again, cutting her off. The kiss didn't feel like pretend. It felt unbearably, unbelievably, oh, so achingly real.

He released her abruptly and took a step back. "Get in bed," he said.

She tried a step backward but grabbed at his arms and gave a shaky laugh. "My knees are so rubbery I can't walk."

He swept her up into his arms, took the couple of steps to the bed and dropped her the last foot onto it. The bed bounced, making the springs squeak.

"Shh! Colt and Jake are on the other side of that wall!"

Gavin sat on the edge of the bed and bounced up and down.

"Don't do that!" she whispered. "My brothers will hear and think we're…we're…"

"Doing it?" he whispered back with a teasing grin.

"Yes!" she hissed, mortified.

He stopped but the grin remained in place. Until his eyes slid down her body to where her rounded stomach was so obviously apparent beneath the clinging silk.

Rolleen watched the grin fade. Watched Gavin rise and take a step or two back from her.

"I'll change when the light's off," he said, "and sleep on the floor."

"We can share—"

"Don't argue with me, Rolleen," he said curtly. "This may be pretend, but you're a woman and I'm a man and I can't help how I react to you—pregnant or not. Now get under the damn covers and turn out the light!"

Rolleen did as she was told.

She heard the zipper come down on Gavin's jeans, and the whispery hush of denim being dropped in a pile. She felt him pick up the extra blanket at her feet and edge away as he confiscated the pillow next to her head.

"You can still join me if you get cold," she offered.

"I won't."

She knew why. He was physically attracted to her. She'd felt it from the beginning. She could understand her attraction to him. He was tall, dark and handsome. She had never understood his apparent attraction to her. She was pretty—but pregnant! That hadn't deterred Gavin's interest in the least. If anything, he had seemed fascinated by her pregnant body. *If only...*

Rolleen made herself face the facts. Gavin Talbot was helping her through a difficult situation. It wasn't fair to either of them to let herself dream of happily ever after.

"Good night, Gavin." She heard him shuffling around on the floor, spreading out the blanket and pounding the pillow and turning himself over several times, until at last he was quiet.

She wanted to stay awake and talk, but it had been such a long day she could hardly keep her eyes open. She was home. Her parents believed their ruse. This Christmas would be as happy as all the others. And Gavin's presence—and his pretense—had made it all possible. She owed him so much.

"Gavin?" Halfway through the word she yawned.

"You're tired. Go to sleep."

"It was perfect, Gavin," she said dreamily. "Everyone around the fire. Everyone smiling and laughing and happy. Just like Christmas should be. Thank you."

"It isn't over yet," he said.

"Only two days until Christmas Eve," she said. "We'll make it."

"Maybe you will," he muttered.

"What?"

"Nothing."

Rolleen laid her hand protectively over the baby, closed her eyes and moments later was sound asleep.

Gavin couldn't remember when he'd spent a more miserable night. His body had been a furnace of desire when he'd lain down on the floor, but during the night, the cold had seeped up through the rug from the Mexican-tiled floor. The blanket had been too short to reach his feet and his shoulders at the same time, and it had taken a great deal of fortitude not to join Rolleen in bed.

To make matters worse, the feather pillow had been too soft and the pillowcase had smelled of honeysuckle, a scent Rolleen sometimes wore. Gavin had spent the night aching for her. If he got involved— really involved—with Rolleen Whitelaw, it meant accepting another man's child as his own. But if he hadn't been able to accept Beth, whom he had adored the first four years of her life, how could he ever hope to love some stranger's child?

He had to make himself stop touching Rolleen. Stop wanting her. Stop thinking about her.

That was easier said than done.

Gavin had awakened at the crack of dawn and retreated to the bathroom across the hall to shower and shave before Rolleen and her family got up. He hadn't wanted to see her all warm and tousled in bed. And he had wanted all the time he could get to gather his courage before he had to face Zach and Rebecca again.

Last night, when Zach had come to the bedroom door, Gavin had imagined how he would have felt if some guy had come to his home "pretending" to love his daughter—who was pregnant—and then abandoned her a couple of months later. No matter when Zach and Rebecca found out the truth, they were going to be angry and hurt.

But he also could understand Rolleen wanting to preserve the joy of Christmas for her family. No matter how hard he was finding it, Gavin owed it to her to try to keep his part of the bargain.

He simply had to stop kissing her like he had last night. Because it was too hard to keep from feeling things he would rather not feel.

Knuckles rapped hard on the bathroom door, and he heard Rabbit call out, "Hey! You done in there?"

He opened the door a crack, shaved but wearing only a pair of half-buttoned jeans.

The fifteen-year-old shot him an aggrieved look and said, "I hope you didn't use all the hot water."

"Rabbit!" Colt said, cuffing his brother on the shoulder as he passed by. "Let the guy finish getting dressed!"

Gavin peered out and realized the hall was alive with Whitelaws coming in and out of bedroom doors in various states of dress and undress. He should have known they'd all keep rancher's hours.

"I'm finished in here," he said, dropping his towel into the hamper and stepping barefoot out into the hall along with a cloud of leftover steam. "I took a quick shower," he promised Rabbit as he headed across the hall to Rolleen's bedroom.

"You're last tomorrow if you didn't," Rabbit threatened as he stepped inside and closed the door behind him.

Gavin felt himself grinning. He'd certainly become one of the family.

The hall was suddenly empty, and Gavin wondered where everyone had gone. He hesitated on the threshold of Rolleen's bedroom, fascinated by what he saw.

Rolleen was sitting up in the big brass bed with both pillows stacked behind her, a saltine cracker poised at her lips, her gray eyes crinkled at the corners and her mouth split wide by laughter. The sound was so beautiful—like twinkling stars in a winter sky or snowfall stacked on the boughs of a mountain pine or children dressed as angels—it took his breath away.

He watched as Rebecca lovingly brushed Rolleen's blond hair away from her face and said, "I don't have any firsthand experience, but all your aunts have told me the first trimester is pretty exhausting. How are you feeling, really?"

Gavin was startled by Rebecca's reminder that none of her children had been born Whitelaws, that every one of them had been adopted. She had learned to love eight children who were not her own.

"I'm fine, Mom. Really," Rolleen said. "And the baby's fine."

Gavin watched as Rolleen took her mother's hand and laid it over her belly where the child was growing inside her. He saw the look of delight on Rebecca's face and the glow that lit Rolleen's and made her every bit as beautiful as her laughter.

"Were you ever sorry, Mom?" Rolleen asked. "I mean, that none of us were your own?"

Gavin listened raptly for Rebecca's answer, knowing he shouldn't be eavesdropping, but unable to move from where he stood.

"I have always wondered what it would be like to feel a child growing inside me," Rebecca admitted. "It must be wonderful to give such a gift to the man you love."

Gavin saw Rolleen's hesitation before she nodded.

"But your father and I have had the unique pleasure of finding each and every one of you children—never knowing when or from where the next would arrive. It's been a life filled with wonderful gifts I wouldn't have missed for anything."

Both women had tears in their eyes, and Gavin wished he could disappear into the wall. He didn't need this. Of course Rebecca could love someone else's children. There was no history of deception, no feelings of betrayal connected to them. His situation with Beth was different. It had been impossible to keep loving Beth once he'd learned his wife had betrayed him in creating her.

In the early days after he had learned the truth about his daughter his grandmother had been the first to say, "People can learn to love children who aren't their own."

"That isn't the point," he'd argued. The part of himself he'd always believed was a part of his daughter no longer existed. Before he'd even had a chance to grieve that loss, he was being asked to love the part of his daughter that was a stranger, along with the part of her that reminded him of a wife who had betrayed him with another man.

So far, he hadn't been able to do it.

"You can't keep ignoring her," his grandmother

had admonished the last time he'd left the ranch to return to Houston. "Take her with you, Gavin. Be her father. Love her. Beth loves you so much! She doesn't understand why you avoid her. She doesn't understand—"

"Please, Hester, no more," he'd said. "I can't face Beth right now and pretend everything is the way it was. I can't."

"You're breaking my heart," Hester had said.

He'd felt the ache in his throat and known he couldn't stay any longer. He had turned to leave the room and collided with Beth.

"Daddy, don't leave me!" she'd cried excitedly, holding her arms open wide to him. "Take me with you!"

His first instinct had been to pick her up, to hold her, to cherish her and protect her from the truth. He had dropped onto one knee and found himself looking into eyes that were not the shape or color of his—or Susan's. Beth's hands were already closing around his neck when he had caught her wrists and pulled himself free. "I can't, baby. I can't!"

She had stared at him confused, but not frightened, because he had always been so gentle with her. "Why not, Daddy?"

I'm not your Daddy.

Dark and dangerous rage. Huge and horrible grief. Aching, unbearable pain. He had felt all of it at once and jerked himself free of its source: his daughter…who was not his daughter.

Gavin had run. And been running for almost a year. At Hester's insistence, he was going home for Christmas. Home to face the blameless child he had abandoned and try to be a father to her.

"Gavin?"

Gavin realized Rebecca and Rolleen had noticed his presence while he'd been lost in thought. "I'm sorry. What did you say?"

Rebecca laughed as she rose from the bed. "I was just saying I ought to excuse myself so you two can finish dressing. We've got a hectic day ahead of us."

She was gone with a smile and a wave, closing him inside the bedroom with Rolleen.

Gavin took one look at Rolleen and felt his body draw up tight. He swore under his breath. He wanted her, but he knew better than to reach for her. The situation was just too damned complicated. He stayed where he was, restraining the hungry beast inside.

"Are you all right?" she asked.

"Why wouldn't I be?" he said, his voice hard and hoarse with desire.

"I know things aren't as private around here as you're used to," she said, putting her feet over the edge of the bed. She rose as though she had a book balanced on her head, and he suspected her stomach was unsteady.

What kind of crazy man craves sex with a woman who has morning sickness? He did. He wanted her something fierce, and she was totally oblivious!

"But we Whitelaws are a close-knit family who—"

"Why don't you tell them the truth?"

She froze, then turned to stare at him. "What?"

"I can see they all love you. They won't blame

you for what happened. Why don't you just tell them the truth and get it over with?''

He watched the blood leech from her face and hurried over to sit her down on the bed and force her head between her knees. ''Keep your head down,'' he said when she tried to raise it too soon.

''Please don't tell them,'' she begged. ''Not now. Not yet.''

He pulled her up and into his arms and hugged her. He felt bad for her and her parents. And helpless because there was nothing he could do to make things better.

Except keep playing the game.

Her hair felt silky in his hands as he tunneled his fingers up the back of her neck to rub at the knots of tension there.

''That feels good.''

The sound of her voice resonated inside him, making his blood race.

''At least tell them you don't mind quitting medical school,'' he said, fighting the urge to crush her against him. ''Will you do that for me?''

''I suppose I could say you're going to encourage me to work on some fashion designs at home,'' she said.

''It'll be the truth,'' he said.

She smiled up at him, and Gavin felt something tumble and shift inside. *It isn't just that I want her body. I want her. I need her.*

''You're a nice man, Gavin Talbot.''

''And a hungry one,'' he said, watching the double entendre slide right over her head. *If only...* He forced himself to let go of her and asked, "When's breakfast?"

"You can eat anytime you want. I'm not having anything."

"Oh, yes you are," he countered. "I want you strong enough to keep up your end of the bargain."

"But I'll be sick if I eat," she protested.

"You can nibble on something."

Nibble was all she did, but he made sure she mentioned her plan to do some fashion designs for The Elegant Lady.

"What a wonderful idea," Rebecca said.

"You've always loved to sew," Jewel pointed out.

"And I've always wanted a sister who was a fashion designer," the irrepressible Frannie said.

"You would," Jake said. "So you can dress up in her clothes."

"What's wrong with that?" Frannie asked indignantly.

Everybody laughed.

Before Gavin knew it the whole family had tumbled out of the kitchen door like kittens out of a basket and were on their way to the stable to take a quick ride around Hawk's Pride.

When the ride became a race, Gavin excused himself and Rolleen, insisting she had promised to take him on a side trip down into the canyon where the stone walls were etched with primitive drawings.

"Thank you, Gavin," Rolleen said once they were on the narrow trail into the canyon.

"For what?"

"For helping me to have faith in my parents," she replied. "I should have known they would be supportive no matter what I chose to do. You'll make a good parent someday yourself.''

Gavin stared at her, stricken. *But I'm not a good parent,* he wanted to shout. *I'm not even in the same class with Zach and Rebecca. They've opened their hearts to eight children who aren't their own flesh and blood. I can't even do it with one.* He glanced at her growing belly, visible in the jeans she wore to ride in, and realized it wasn't only one child he needed to love anymore. It was two.

He wanted to talk with Rolleen about Beth, to seek her advice, to seek solace, but once he had her alone at the bottom of the canyon, he couldn't help tasting her. And tasting led to touching.

He kissed the curls on her nape and the small birthmark he'd found beneath her ear, and he put his palms over her breasts and heard her moan as the nipples peaked.

''Gavin, please stop.''

Through a haze of arousal he heard her plea. And did as she asked.

''Your brothers will expect you to look kissed,'' he said.

She was flushed, her cheeks rosy, her lips swollen from his kisses. But her gray eyes were troubled.

''We have to stop this, Gavin.''

He didn't pretend to misunderstand her. ''I like kissing you, Rolleen. And touching you.'' He brushed the back of his hand against her breast, and she hissed in a breath.

''I don't want to get hurt, Gavin. I'm starting to feel things…things I shouldn't feel for you. It doesn't feel like a game anymore,'' she said.

"Maybe it isn't," he murmured.

"What?"

"Maybe it doesn't have to be," he said, meeting her startled gaze. "What if we kept on seeing each other after the holidays?"

She stared up at him, her heart in her eyes for a brief moment before she turned away. "I...I don't know." She turned back to him and said, "I'll think about it."

Her brothers ribbed her unmercifully for her bright eyes and swollen lips and heated cheeks when they rejoined the rest of the party and Gavin made himself smile along with them, while inside it felt like someone had dumped the spoon drawer upside down, causing a great clatter and a great deal of confusion.

I never told her about Beth, he realized. *I have to tell her about Beth.*

After lunch they played flag football. The third time Rolleen got tackled by one of her brothers, Gavin picked her up and sat her in a chair on the stone patio behind the house and ordered in a very husbandly way, "Stay there and take care of our baby."

In the late afternoon Gavin volunteered to help chop more wood for the fire along with Rolleen's brothers. He almost cut his foot off when Rolleen cried out because a lizard had crawled across her boot. Her brothers razzed him unmercifully for not being able to take his eyes off of her.

He punished Rolleen for scaring him with a kiss in front of her brothers that left her cheeks pink. She got him back by threading her fingers into his hair and ravaging his mouth with her tongue until his jeans barely fit. He had to stand behind the woodpile until he was decent, while she smiled smugly and trotted off to the house with her sisters.

It was fun. The rambunctious activities went on for the next two days, with Rolleen notably absent for the rougher games and with the family joined by Rolleen's sister Cherry, her husband Billy, their twin ten-year-old daughters Rae Jean and Annie and the new baby Brett. Gavin didn't know when he'd enjoyed the Christmas holiday so much.

Rolleen laughed often and unselfconsciously. She teased and cajoled and got angry with her brothers and sisters and forgave them minutes later. She teased and cajoled and got angry with him, too. And forgave him with touches and kisses and looks that made his blood simmer beneath his skin.

His feelings felt like love. But he was always aware of the deception they carried out with her parents, always aware of the secret he kept from her that might make her turn away from him.

The more Gavin watched the loving play of the Whitelaws, the more time he spent with Rolleen, the more he dreaded the thought of leaving Hawk's Pride and heading for his home to play out the rest of their charade.

The moment came much sooner than he expected. And in a way that made it plain how much was at stake in the dangerous game they played.

Chapter 6

Rolleen had let herself enjoy the days before Christmas without thinking about the future. But she was troubled by Gavin's offer to extend their make-believe relationship beyond the holidays. She was afraid to believe he loved her, afraid to believe she could be in love again so soon. She had made one mistake. She didn't want to make another.

"What are you doing hiding out here while everyone's inside?"

Rolleen scooted over in the wooden front porch swing that hung from the rafters and made room for her mother under the quilt she'd brought outside to keep herself warm. Then she started the swing moving again with her toe. "I wanted some peace and quiet to think before we leave for the Christmas Eve candlelight service," she said.

They both listened to the lonely sounds of the prairie. The screech of a windmill that always needed more oil. The soft lowing of cattle. The rustle of leaves in the giant live oak. The whisper of the wind through the buffalo grass.

"Gavin's a good man, Rolleen," her mother said.

"I know he is, Mom." Rolleen avoided meeting her mother's glance, afraid her mom would read the doubts there—or see the deception.

"Then why haven't you married him?"

"There are some things we need to work out," she hedged.

"Your father and I love you, darling, and we're behind you, no matter what course you choose. I know how hard it is for you to give your trust to anyone. But sometimes—"

"I'm afraid," Rolleen blurted.

She felt her mother's arm slide around her shoulder and laid her head against her mother's breast.

"What if I make the wrong choice, Mom? What if I mess up my life and the baby's?"

"Shh. Shh," her mother crooned. "Listen to your heart and believe in yourself and you'll know what to do."

Her mother hadn't offered a solution to Rolleen's dilemma, only love and trust and the belief that Rolleen could solve the problem herself. It was what she had always given. It was everything a child could want or need.

"Thank you, Mom," she said.

"Anytime, darling. Will you come inside now?"

"In a little while," she said as her mother stepped inside the house.

When Gavin showed up on the porch a few moments after her mother had gone inside, he said, ''I've been looking everywhere for you. Rebecca said I'd find you out here. I was worried about you. Why aren't you inside with your family?''

He didn't wait for her to invite him under the blanket. He simply lifted it and her and sat himself down with her in his lap.

She laughed and rearranged the blanket over both of them. ''You're getting good at that.''

''It's going to get tougher as you get bigger with—''

''The baby,'' they both said together and laughed.

''Why can't it be like this the whole year long?'' Rolleen said.

''Like what?''

''Everyone so happy, so generous and considerate and kind.''

''I suppose there's no reason why it can't be like that,'' Gavin said, setting the hanging rocker in motion.

''I wish…''

''What do you wish?''

''I wish this were your baby.''

His harsh intake of breath, the tension in his thighs beneath her and the stiffness in his shoulder under her hand all told a story much louder than words. She wished the baby were his. He obviously did not.

''Rolleen, I—''

She put her fingertips over his mouth to stop his denial. ''You don't have to say anything, Gavin. It isn't your baby. It isn't your responsibility. I appreciate what you've done so far, and I won't expect anything from you once the holidays are over, I promise.''

He grabbed her hand and pulled it away. ''Rolleen, damn it, there's a lot you don't know about me. Things I haven't told you that are important—that make a difference!''

''It doesn't matter. None of it matters!'' She was up and off his lap a second later, running for the front door. She pulled it open and found herself in the midst of a free-for-all in the living room.

She stopped stock-still in the doorway and stared at Jake and Colt and Frannie and Cherry and Mac and Billy. She and the baby would manage without Gavin. She might not be as happy, but she would be all right. She had her family to love—and to love her.

''Hey, Rolleen,'' Frannie shouted, pointing upward. ''Look where you're standing!''

Rolleen saw the sprig of mistletoe at the same time Gavin slipped his arms around her from behind.

''You have to kiss Gavin!'' Frannie said, her voice laced with adolescent relish for all things romantic.

The family began to laugh and clap, making it impossible for her to escape without making a scene. It should have been the simplest thing in the world to turn around and kiss Gavin. She had been kissing him for days in front of her family. But now she knew her dreams of happily-ever-after were nothing more than that. Now she knew this fairy tale was not going to have a happy ending.

She didn't want to pretend with Gavin anymore. When she hesitated, Gavin questioned, ''Rolleen?''

''Kiss me, Gavin,'' she whispered. ''Kiss me one last time.''

* * *

Gavin heard the cheers as he leaned down to touch his lips to Rolleen's. His heart was thundering in his chest, and it hurt to breathe. He wanted her so much. *He loved her so much.*

Gavin ended the kiss and stared stunned at Rolleen for an instant. *I love her.* "Rolleen..."

The room was suddenly silent. Gavin could almost feel her family willing Rolleen to accept him and set a date for the wedding.

I'm not acting, Rolleen. I do care for you. But in this case, loving her was not enough. He must also be able to love her child. And his own.

The phone in the kitchen rang, but no one left the room to answer it.

Gavin saw the troubled look in Rolleen's eyes and knew what had put it there. She had wished her baby was his. She had offered him that precious gift—a child of hers—and he had not been able to accept it. What was wrong with him? Why couldn't he love them both?

Then Gavin realized the enormity of the harm he had done by wanting more than the game allowed. There was more in her eyes than regret. There was love.

Oh, God, Rolleen. I'm so sorry. I never meant for this to happen.

"I—I—think..." she stuttered. She turned and stared at the kitchen doorway. "Shouldn't someone answer that phone?"

"Set a date! Set a date!" Frannie chanted.

"Frannie," Rebecca chided lovingly. "Give Rolleen a chance to speak for herself. Get the phone please, Jewel.''

"Don't say anything till I get back,'' Jewel shouted to Rolleen as she raced to the kitchen. "I don't want to miss this!''

Everyone groaned.

Jewel quickly returned from the kitchen and extended the portable phone to Gavin. "It's for you, a friend of your grandmother's named Ruby Jenkins. She says your grandmother's ill. She said you should come home right away and bring someone to take care of your daughter.''

Gavin felt every pair of eyes in the room focus on him. He knew they were all wondering why he had never mentioned a daughter. He clutched Rolleen's hands to keep her from jerking away, turned to her family and said, "I'm sorry, Zach, Rebecca, everybody. I'm afraid Rolleen and I are going to have to cut our visit short. My daughter can be a handful.''

Gavin held his breath. It was up to Rolleen now. She could either call everything off, or come along with him.

He looked into Rolleen's eyes and winced when he saw her pain and confusion. He should have told her sooner. He had thought he would have more time. Only, time had run out.

"I have to leave, Rolleen. Are you coming with me?''

Are you going to keep your part of the bargain?

Gavin didn't say those precise words, but Rolleen heard them. She felt like Alice, and she'd just fallen down the rabbit's hole into Wonderland, where nothing was as it seemed.

But she knew for sure now that Gavin hadn't really wanted her to set a date. Not when she knew nothing about the existence of his daughter. She realized how close she had let herself come to believing in happily ever after. She had to remember the rules of this game.

She felt both angry and hurt at Gavin's secretiveness. Realistically, there was no way she and Gavin could have learned everything about each other in two weeks. But a *daughter* was a pretty sizable omission.

Why hadn't he told her about the child? What was wrong with her? Was she sick? Dying? Was that why Gavin counseled dying children? Rolleen wanted answers, and the only way she was going to get them was to go with him.

She turned to her parents and said, "Momma, Daddy, I'm sorry to leave like this, but I need to go with Gavin. I should have told you sooner, but I'd planned all along to spend part of the holiday with his family. We'll just be leaving a little sooner than we'd planned."

"We'll miss having you here," her mother said.

The concern on her parents' faces made her want to confess everything, but so far Christmas had been wonderful. She wanted to leave her family with that lovely feeling.

Rolleen smiled, a look she hoped conveyed her gratefulness to her parents and her love for them. "I'll be fine, Mom. I'll call you when we get there. Merry Christmas, Daddy. Merry Christmas, everybody!"

Rolleen felt herself being moved through the room

by Gavin's strong arm around her waist as her family reached out to wish her well, her brothers shouting, "Merry Christmas, Gavin!" and her sisters saying, "Call as soon as you can, Rolleen!" and "Let us know how your grandmother is, Gavin!"

Rolleen hugged her parents hard and watched from the corner of her eye as Gavin shook her father's hand and said soberly, "Don't worry, sir. I'll take care of her."

Rolleen said nothing while she and Gavin packed their bags. She kept her silence as they drove to the airport and turned in the rental car. She waited patiently, biding her time until they were several thousand feet in the air where Gavin couldn't escape, before she began asking for answers.

"Tell me about your daughter."

He avoided her gaze. "What would you like to know?"

"How old is she? What's her name? Why have you kept her a secret?"

"She'll be five on January 22. Her name's Elizabeth Harriet Talbot, Beth for short. And I haven't mentioned her before because…she's the real reason I wanted you to come home with me this Christmas."

Rolleen brushed a nervous hand through her hair. "Well. That sounds like the truth, at least."

"I've never lied to you, Rolleen," he said.

"But you edited something pretty important out of your life, Gavin. What else have you kept a secret that I ought to know about?"

She heard the gusty sigh and knew there was more. "You don't have to worry that you're going to be obligated to me beyond the holidays," she said.

He turned sharply to look at her, then said, "When my wife died, she left a note telling me that Beth isn't my daughter."

Rolleen felt an ache in her chest at Gavin's revelation. She didn't know what to say. "I'm sorry," didn't seem like enough. "How awful!" sounded wrong. And any comment about his wife's behavior was too judgmental, when she knew nothing about their life together.

"You must have been devastated," she said at last.

"It hasn't been an easy year," he conceded. "I've gone home to visit Beth more this fall than I did in the spring, but I haven't been able to look at my daughter without..." He swallowed hard before continuing, "Without thinking about who her father might be. Without imagining... I've done my best not to let on to Beth how I feel. But it isn't easy when she wants me to hold her, and..." He swallowed hard again but said nothing more.

"I'm sorry," she said.

When Rolleen had been silent for several minutes, Gavin said, "Aren't you going to ask me anything else?"

"I don't want to cause you any more pain," she admitted.

He opened his mouth but closed it again without speaking.

She turned to look at him and waited.

"I can't..." He huffed out a breath and said, "I don't feel the same way toward Beth that I did before...before."

"I don't understand," she said. "Are you saying you blame Beth for what her mother did?"

"I don't love her anymore," he said flatly. "I can't bear to look at her. I don't want to be in the same room with her. Is that what you wanted to hear?"

He was breathing hard, as though he'd been running, but Gavin was still sitting in the same pilot's seat where he'd been when he'd started talking. He gave a ragged sigh. "I feel a tremendous responsibility toward Beth, but that's all. My grandmother can't seem to grasp the fact that my feelings have changed."

"What is my presence supposed to accomplish?" Rolleen asked.

"I figured if you were there Hester would understand why I'd rather be with you than with Beth and wouldn't be throwing me and Beth together so much."

"Is that what she does? Throw you and Beth together?"

Gavin scowled. "All the time!"

"From that phone call you got, it sounds like she'll likely be in bed sick and not bothering anybody."

"Hester's a sturdy old bird," he said. "Nothing keeps her down for very long. Believe me, she'll be back to her old, interfering self in no time."

"You could at least play with Beth while your grandmother's sick, couldn't you?"

He shook his head. "No. No, I couldn't."

Rolleen was trying to understand, and she was afraid she did. Her white knight's armor was beginning to look a little tarnished.

"I was adopted, Gavin, so I know adults can learn to love children who aren't their own. Couldn't you try that with Beth? Couldn't you pretend she's a child you found in an orphanage and learn to love her all over again?''

"But she isn't!" he snarled. "Every time she smiles I see my wife's smile. And every time I look into her eyes I see some stranger—some man who took my wife to bed—looking back at me!"

Gavin was shaking with anger. Rolleen had the feeling that if he'd been in a boxing ring he would happily have pulverized his opponent. If he'd been on the road, he might have rammed the nearest tree. Fortunately they were up in the air with nothing to run into but a bank of clouds and plenty of sky in which to maneuver.

Rolleen was trying to understand and appreciate and sympathize with Gavin's pain. Instead she found herself wearing Beth's shoes, because she'd worn them once herself and because she knew how much they hurt.

"Have you thought about what Beth must be feeling?" she asked.

"She's just a kid," Gavin said.

"Kids have feelings. At least I did."

She watched the frown burrow deep into Gavin's forehead. He didn't answer her, but she knew she'd made her point.

"You should have told me what you had in mind from the beginning," she said. "I could have told you then I couldn't be a part of it."

He turned to stare at her in disbelief. "What?"

"I couldn't possibly help you ignore your daughter just because she isn't your own flesh and blood, Gavin. I've been where she is. I've felt what she's feeling. Once we get on the ground, I'll find my own way back to Houston.''

"I helped you out," he said furiously. "I gave you the Christmas you wanted. Now it's your turn. We made a bargain, Rolleen. And I'm not letting you out of it!"

"I won't go off with you and ignore Beth," she retorted, just as heatedly.

"Fine. Play games with her. Talk to her. Do anything you want with her. Just keep her away from me!"

Rolleen stared at Gavin, appalled at what he was saying. She had felt herself falling in love with him during the time they'd spent at Hawk's Pride, but she realized now what a good thing it was she hadn't said anything. He had let her down, but she wasn't going to let his daughter suffer as a consequence. That little girl was going to get the love she deserved at Christmas.

"All right," Rolleen said. "I'll come home with you."

"As my fiancée?" Gavin asked.

"Is that really necessary? Couldn't I just be your friend?"

He hesitated and shook his head. "I don't think so. I want the same thing for Hester that you wanted for your mom and dad. My grandmother doesn't have a lot of Christmases left, and I want this one to be happy for her."

"And seeing you engaged will make her happy?"

"Having me married would make her a lot happier," Gavin said, "but this is as far as I'm willing to go. Hester's afraid I won't be able to love another woman after what happened with Susan. You'll be proof that isn't the case.''

''What happens when we don't get married?''

''I could ask you the same question.''

They sat in silence thinking about what they'd done. Realizing what they'd wrought.

Rolleen wondered if Gavin could love another woman. Wondered if he could love his child. Wondered if he could love hers. She had to admit she still fantasized about a future with him. Foolish woman. That really was living in Wonderland.

''What were we thinking?'' she muttered, shaking her head.

''We weren't,'' he said flatly.

Runway landing lights appeared in the distance. ''Where are we?'' she asked.

''That's a private air strip on my ranch,'' he said.

''This is your ranch?'' she said, perusing the vast rolling hills studded with an occasional live oak that were visible in the pink light of Christmas morning.

''We've been flying over it for the past half hour.''

Rolleen stared at him. ''All that land was yours?''

He nodded. ''The Lady Luck has been in the Talbot family for generations.''

''I see,'' she murmured, realizing for the first time that if the Lady Luck went to Beth, it would be going to someone who was not a Talbot. ''It's beautiful,'' she conceded.

''Yes,'' he said, his voice as soft and reverent as she had ever heard it. ''It is.''

The two-engine plane bounced and skidded as the wheels settled on terra firma, and an old army jeep began following them down the runway.

"Thanks, Rolleen," Gavin said as the plane slowed to a halt.

"Don't thank me yet," she said as a hired hand opened the plane door for her. "Let's wait until I meet your grandmother—and your daughter—and see if I can go through with this."

Chapter 7

Rolleen was enchanted by the Lady Luck ranch house. "It's made of logs, like the ranch houses in the movies!"

Gavin grinned and said, "My great-great-grandfather came from Kentucky. He didn't want a Spanish hacienda or some southern plantation home. He wanted a simple log cabin, and that's what he built."

"Simple?" she said, cocking a brow in disbelief.

Maybe a primitive log cabin was what Gavin's ancestor had built, but generations of Talbots had obviously added to the place, making it a delightful hodgepodge of levels and sending it in several directions. The massive ranch house and rustic outbuildings sprawled across one of the rolling hills she'd seen from the sky, shaded by immense, tangled live oaks.

She and Gavin had stripped down to T-shirts and jeans to accommodate the warmer South Texas weather and left their coats and sweaters and suitcases in the jeep. But Rolleen had insisted Gavin bring in the shopping bag full of Christmas gifts, since her parents had added a few last-minute items for Beth from the gifts they'd intended for Cherry's twin girls.

"Your home is beautiful," Rolleen said to Gavin as they stepped onto the wooden covered porch in back.

"Thanks. Seeing it through your eyes, I can appreciate how unique it really is."

The back door was open, and in the early-morning quiet, Rolleen could hear someone humming, "She'll be Comin' Round the Mountain." It wasn't a Christmas tune, but it somehow fit the log cabin setting and made Rolleen smile. She sniffed, smelled yeast and said, "Someone's baking."

"That'll be Hester."

"But she's ill."

"Not too sick to bake, apparently. I'd recognize that smell anywhere. Hester makes the same breakfast every Christmas morning—the most delicious glazed pecan rolls you ever ate in your life. The pecans come from trees here on the Lady Luck planted by my grandfather, just so my grandmother would always be sure to have pecans on Christmas morning."

The screen door squealed as Gavin pulled it open, and Rolleen got her first look at his grandmother.

"Gavin! What a surprise!" she said, her face splitting wide with a smile as Gavin ushered Rolleen inside. "We didn't expect you before noon!"

Hester Talbot didn't look seventy-three—or the

least bit sick. She was tall, slim and wiry, like some pioneer woman, her silver-gray hair in a bun at her crown, wisps of it escaping at her temples to frame a face given character by the lines etched on it. Her dark eyes were bright with interest, and her step—she was dressed in a Western plaid shirt, jeans and boots—was lively.

"Who's this?" Hester asked, her features curious but friendly as she examined Rolleen.

"Why aren't you in bed?" Gavin asked, giving his grandmother a hug so warm he looked like a bear who'd found a honey pot. "You're supposed to be sick."

"Why would you think a fool thing like that?"

"Because Ruby Jenkins called and said you were."

"I'll dangle that woman from her own telephone pole some day, see if I don't!" Hester said, shaking her head. "I told her I had the *sniffles!* As you can see, I'm fit as a fiddle. Or will be, when you tell me who this is you've brought home for Christmas."

"I'll be glad to, as soon as I can get a word in edgewise," Gavin said with a laugh.

Hester apparently couldn't wait. "I'm Hester Talbot," she volunteered, holding out her hand in welcome.

"Rolleen Whitelaw," Rolleen said, surprised at the strength of Hester's grip and the hard calluses she felt against her palm. The shrewd appraisal in the older woman's eyes made her heart thump a little faster. It wasn't going to be easy deceiving this woman. Hester Talbot was nobody's fool.

For the first time, Rolleen realized how Gavin must have felt meeting her parents and knowing he was only playing a role. She opened her mouth to tell the truth, but Gavin spoke first.

"Rolleen and I are engaged," he said, slipping his arm around Rolleen's waist and giving her a playfully smacking but startlingly sensual kiss.

"Stop that right now, Gavin Talbot. You're embarrassing the poor girl!" Hester ordered. Only, it was plain from the heightened color on Hester's cheeks, she was the one who needed rescue. "I'm so pleased for both of you," she said, waiting until Gavin let go of Rolleen to give her a hug. "I see you're wearing the Talbot diamond."

"You don't mind, do you?"

Hester snorted. "Mind? That diamond only fits the women Talbot men are supposed to wed. It's sort of like Cinderella's slipper. Can't be sized, don't you know? Didn't fit Susan," she said with a significant glance at Gavin. "Fits you fine, though."

Rolleen stared at Gavin, wondering why he hadn't filled her in on that little bit of Talbot folklore. "I see," she said.

Gavin sniffed the air and said, "How long before those famous pecan rolls of yours come out of the oven?"

Rolleen saw the pleasure on Hester's face at Gavin's eagerness to sample her wares.

"No more than ten minutes, maybe less. Promised Beth she could have them with her bacon and eggs. Child could hardly sleep last night, knowing we'd be opening presents this morning. She's been fondling that package you sent her last week like it was a real baby and not a doll—and don't ask how I know you got her one. I expect having you here'll be all the present that girl really needs.''

Rolleen had been watching the byplay between grandmother and grandson, finding comfort in the evident love between them. So she saw the way Gavin tensed at the mention of his daughter. It was plain he wasn't looking forward to the meeting as much as Beth apparently was.

''Beth!'' Hester said. ''How long have you been standing there, girl? Come and say hello to your daddy.''

Rolleen turned and saw a rail-thin little girl in the doorway staring at them from large, anxious wide-set eyes, one bare foot atop the other, wearing a puffy-sleeved, flower-patterned nightgown with a ruffle at the hem.

She held tight to the door frame with her right hand, while her left forefinger twined nervously around a strand of her short black hair, which was parted in the middle and came to her chin, framing her face. Her upturned nose held a spattering of freckles, and her eyes—an unusual gray-green color—looked warily back at Rolleen from beneath long black lashes.

''Come on over here, and give your father a hug,'' Hester encouraged the little girl.

To Rolleen's surprise, instead of running toward her father, Beth scampered to her grandmother, hiding behind Hester's Levi's and peering out at her father.

The yearning look on Beth's face was as heartbreaking as the tight-lipped look on Gavin's. The thick lump in Rolleen's throat came without warning.

Before it had eased enough for her to speak, the oven timer buzzed.

"My pecan rolls are ready," Hester announced. "Why don't you take Beth and get her dressed while I take them out of the oven," Hester said to Gavin.

Rolleen was afraid Gavin was going to refuse, and she couldn't bear to see the little girl hurt. "Would you mind if I came along?" she said to Beth.

Beth looked anxiously from Rolleen to her father. "My daddy says I'm not supposed to go with strangers."

Rolleen turned to Gavin. The next move was his. She begged him with her eyes to make the right one.

"Rolleen's a friend of mine," he said to Beth. "If it's all right with you, I'd like her to come along."

"Okay, Daddy. She can come." Beth held out her hand to Rolleen and said, "Come with me, and I'll show you where my bedroom is."

Rolleen looked over her shoulder and met Gavin's eyes as Beth drew her down the hall. *All she wants is to be loved. That isn't so hard, is it?*

Apparently, it was. Gavin followed them, but from the sour look on his face he might have been the guest of honor at a western necktie party—the kind where the guest was left hanging when everybody else went home.

The furnishings in Gavin's home reflected as many different periods and styles as the outside of the house and Rolleen was enchanted by the whimsical nature of the decorations. A 1920's era lady's cloche hat hung on an eighteenth-century mirrored hall tree, and a man's cherry-wood humidor sat on a delicate marble armoire. The ranch house was filled with museum pieces, but it had a lived-in look.

"I love your home, Gavin," Rolleen said. She stopped at Beth's doorway and gasped in delight. "Your bed looks like a covered wagon!"

The twin bed had wheels at the four corners, and instead of a traditional canopy, the top was made of white canvas and was shaped in an oval like the top of a western covered wagon.

"This was my daddy's bed, too," Beth said proudly.

Rolleen watched as Gavin lovingly ran a hand over the carved wooden footboard and confessed, "My grandfather made it for me."

While Gavin was admiring the bed, Beth had gone straight to her chest of drawers. She took out a matching shorts set and a pair of socks and without further ado began tugging her nightgown off over her head.

"May I help?" Rolleen asked, crossing to her.

Beth's face appeared in the neck of the nightgown wearing a surprised expression. It was apparent the little girl was used to fending for herself. "Okay," she said.

Rolleen sat down on the edge of the bed and pulled the nightgown the rest of the way over Beth's head, then began helping her into the T-shirt. Once it was on, she helped pull on Beth's shorts over her underwear, then sat the child in her lap to put on her socks.

Rolleen was aware of Gavin standing by, his hands in his pockets, shifting his weight from foot to foot. He appeared ready to bolt at the first opportunity.

"You can put on Beth's left shoe while I get this other sock on," she suggested.

He made a quick face, but knelt in front of them with a pair of pink tennis shoes in hand.

"You have to untie two knots, Daddy," Beth said. "'Cause I tied them like you showed me."

"I see," he said, working on the knots without looking at his daughter.

Beth sat perfectly still and pointed her toe as her father slipped the first shoe on.

He tied the lace, double knotted it and asked, "Is that too tight?"

"Nope." She pointed the other stockinged foot in his direction, and he slipped the other tennis shoe on.

It was obvious to Rolleen, when they both hesitated after Gavin had finished tying Beth's shoes, that there was some ritual they usually performed at this point. She waited to see if Gavin would follow through with it.

Hesitantly he held his arms out to Beth. As she leaped into his embrace, he lifted her high into the air and swung her around and said, "She can leap tall buildings in a single bound!"

Beth shrieked with fear and delight. "Superwoman!"

Rolleen laughed. "Superwoman wears pink tennis shoes?"

"There used to be a pink towel that went with the outfit," Gavin said sheepishly as he set Beth back on the ground.

"Come on, Daddy! Let's eat breakfast, so we can open presents," Beth said, grabbing her father's hand and tugging him toward the door.

Rolleen gave Gavin a supporting look as she followed him out of the bedroom. *That wasn't so bad, was it?* she asked with her eyes.

But his gaze, when Rolleen managed to catch it at the breakfast table, was troubled as he watched his daughter chatter with her grandmother.

Rolleen couldn't have said why it was so important to her that Gavin accept his daughter, and not just accept her, but love her wholeheartedly again. Maybe it was because she had been rejected as a child herself and knew what it felt like to walk in those tiny shoes. And maybe it had something to do with the hope that refused to die inside her that she and Gavin might someday be more than good friends.

She might love Gavin, she was almost certain she already did, but if he couldn't love her unborn child, there was no future for the two of them. However, if Gavin could learn to love Beth again, there was hope he could learn to love the child growing inside her.

Rolleen was putting her faith in the power of love. It could heal all wounds. It was the source of all joy. And if ever there was a time when love abounded, Christmas was the season for it.

Gavin's daughter had trouble sitting still at the breakfast table, she was so excited, and the instant Beth had taken the last bite of food on her plate she asked, "Can we open presents now?"

The little girl bounced her way into the living room, with Rolleen and Gavin and Hester following behind. She dropped to her knees on the rug beside the Christmas tree, her eyes going wide at the sight of the shopping bag full of presents Rolleen had brought along.

"Whose presents are those?" Beth asked, turning to her father.

Rolleen sat down cross-legged beside Beth and said, "I brought them." She reached into the bag and came out with a gaily wrapped present. She checked the tag and said, "This one's for your daddy."

She saw Gavin's startled look from the couch, where he had taken up residence. "I wasn't expecting anything."

"I know," she said with a smile as she handed it over to him. "But I had fun coming up with a present for you."

"Open it, Daddy!" Beth urged, bouncing up and down in place. "Open it!"

"Well, open it, boy!" Hester said, from her comfortable seat on a cushioned wooden rocker by the fireplace. "We want to see what it is."

Rolleen suddenly felt nervous. "I wasn't sure what to get for you so I—"

"Whatever it is will be—" Gavin stopped in mid-speech and stared at her gift.

"What is it, Daddy?" Beth asked, jumping up and crossing to him to get a better look.

Gavin was so absorbed by what he held, Rolleen realized he hadn't even noticed Beth was standing beside him, her hand on his knee. As close together as their faces were, Rolleen could see the child had none of her father's features. Apparently Susan hadn't been lying when she'd told Gavin the child wasn't his. But the longer Rolleen watched, the more similarities between the two she noticed.

Beth tilting her head as Gavin did when he was studying something intently. Beth pointing at the gift with two fingers, instead of one, the way Gavin had on occasion. Beth's brow furrowing with concentration, mirroring the look on her father's face.

Gavin stared at the small, oddly shaped, beribboned, cork-stoppered bottle, looked up at Rolleen and said, "What is it?"

Rolleen laughed and crossed to sit beside him on the couch, pulling Beth into her lap. "The bottle contains salt water and sand from the beach where we had our picnic at Padre Island. It can be a paperweight or—"

Gavin cut her off with a hard kiss on the mouth. "Thanks, Rolleen."

Beth was off her lap in the next instant and running for the shopping bag to pull out another gift, leaving Rolleen still staring at Gavin. "I thought you might like a memento—"

He kissed her again with enough passion to leave her breathless, then turned to his grandmother, held it up and said, "It's love in a bottle."

Rolleen's heart was in her throat. She had felt that way when she put the gift together for him. She hadn't realized it would be so obvious to him. She felt self-conscious having him make such a pronouncement to his grandmother, considering the circumstances.

"What a lovely gift," Hester said to her. "Just the sort of thing a prospective bride ought to give her husband."

Rolleen felt her stomach roll. *Not now. Please, not now.* She swallowed once, twice, then said, "Gavin!"

He took one look at her, bolted to his feet, grabbed her hand and raced for the closest bathroom.

"What's wrong with Rolleen?" Beth cried.

"She's going to have a baby!" Gavin said as he raced by.

"Right now?" Beth called after him.

Over Gavin's shoulder, Rolleen saw the worried look on Hester's face as she called Beth to her side and said, "No, not right now."

Rolleen felt better after she emptied her stomach, but as she lay on the bed in Gavin's bedroom with a cool, wet cloth over her forehead, she wondered what Gavin was telling his grandmother. Revealing her pregnancy to Hester had been no part of their plan, although she supposed they should have realized she might get sick—as she had.

Rolleen heard a soft knock on the door and Hester called, "May I come in?"

She sat up too quickly, saw spots and laid back down before she said, "Please do. I'm sorry to be such a bother," she apologized as Hester crossed the room.

"Are you feeling better?" the older woman said as she sat beside Rolleen on the bed.

"I sat up too quickly just now, but I'm almost as good as new," Rolleen said, as she tried again, sitting up slowly and carefully. She saw Hester glance at her stomach, gauging how far along she was, and said, "The baby's due in May."

"You two planning to get hitched before then?"

Rolleen felt the blood race to her head, heating her cheeks. "We haven't set a date yet."

"You couldn't do much better than that boy," Hester said. "He's a good man. And a good father. Leastwise, he was before that woman he was married to broke his heart.''

"You don't have to tell me Gavin's a wonderful man," Rolleen said. "I've seen it for myself."

"Then why haven't you been to see a preacher?"

Rolleen threaded her fingers together to keep herself from fidgeting and stared at them as though they held the answer she sought. She sighed, looked up at Hester and said, "This isn't Gavin's baby."

"And you're worried he won't be able to love it as much as a father ought to," Hester speculated.

Rolleen nodded.

"I can see where you might think that, seeing how that fool boy has been acting toward his own child."

"His own child?" Rolleen questioned.

"Same as," Hester said. "Might not be his blood running in that child's veins, but Beth's his all right. Take one look at the two of them together—I watched you do it—and a body can't doubt they're closer than a man and his shadow."

Gavin doesn't think he can love Beth anymore. That's why he brought me along. Rolleen thought it, but she couldn't bring herself to say it. She owed that much to Gavin. "Gavin doesn't seem very comfortable around Beth," she said instead.

Hester made a snorting sound. "That woman he was married to left him twisted up a bit inside. You trust that boy. He'll work it out." Hester rose and said, "You feel like joining us again?"

Rolleen swung her feet onto the floor and said, "Of course. I feel fine now."

Rolleen found Gavin sitting with Beth in his lap on the living room couch, reading her Charles Dickens's

A Christmas Carol from a worn, leather-covered book.

"Tradition," Hester whispered in her ear.

The little girl was leaning back against Gavin's chest, twirling a strand of black hair and listening intently as Gavin read the story of Bob Cratchit and Tiny Tim, of Ebenezer Scrooge and the ghosts of Christmases past, present and future. Beth held an oblong wrapped Christmas package curled in her arm as though it were a baby, and Rolleen realized it must be the doll that Gavin had sent to her for Christmas, still unopened.

Rolleen settled on the couch beside Gavin, while Hester sat down once more in the rocker beside the fire. They listened, with only an occasional snap and pop from the wood on the fire as Gavin read about the power of the Christmas spirit to turn selfishness to generosity.

"A Merry Christmas, uncle! God save you!" Gavin read. And then Scrooge's reply, "Bah! Humbug!"

Gavin made the chains rattle when the ghosts appeared to teach Scrooge a lesson and used a falsetto every time he became Tiny Tim.

"A Merry Christmas, Bob!" Gavin said at last, as a reformed Scrooge greeted Bob Cratchit. He finished the story, all except the last line, then stopped and waited while Beth chirped happily, "And God bless Us, Every One!"

Rolleen and Hester clapped. Rolleen smiled but her throat tightened with emotion as she watched Gavin brush Beth's bangs out of her eyes.

Beth looked up at her father and said, "Can I open my present now, Daddy?"

"Sure, pumpkin," he said.

"I'm not a—"

"Pumpkin," they said together with a laugh as he hugged her tight.

Rolleen met Gavin's eyes with tears in her own, and his face sobered. He hadn't needed her here, after all. It hadn't taken much more than the Christmas spirit to reunite Gavin with his daughter. He had never really stopped loving her.

The ribbon on Beth's present went flying, and she ripped the paper with both hands, exposing the colorful cardboard box beneath. There, staring through a cellophane covering, was a Baby Walks and Talks. Reverently Beth removed the doll from the box. It had blond hair and blue eyes and looked nothing at all like Beth. Yet Beth treated the doll as though she had borne it herself. There was a lesson there, Rolleen thought with an inward smile.

Beth pulled the ring that made the doll talk, and it said, "I love you, Mommy."

Beth beamed. She pulled the string again, and the doll said, "I'm hungry." Beth frowned and said, "Where's her bottle, Daddy? Mary's hungry."

"Bottle?" he asked, confused.

"Look in the box," Beth commanded.

Gavin searched the box and found the empty baby bottle and gave it to Beth.

"She needs some milk, Daddy."

"Let's go see what we can find in the kitchen," Hester said, rising and reaching out to take Beth's hand. "You two keep on opening presents. We'll be back in a minute."

"I have something for you, too," Gavin said to Rolleen, once his grandmother was gone.

"What is it?" Rolleen asked.

"Close your eyes."

Rolleen closed them, grinned and said, "I love surprises."

"I know," Gavin replied. His hands moved her hair aside, and she could feel his breath on her temple. "Be still, you're wiggling."

It was the shiver down her spine. What did he expect when he was touching her like that? "What are you doing?"

"Be still so I can finish. You can open them now."

Rolleen opened her eyes and felt around her neck. She lifted the slight gold chain and followed it to the end where a diamond lay in the center of a gold heart. "Oh, Gavin…"

"Do you like it?"

He looked so uncertain, she threw herself into his arms and hugged him hard around the neck. "It's beautiful. And so romantic!" she said with a laugh.

"I wanted to say thanks," he whispered in her ear. "I wanted to tell you how much I've enjoyed the past two weeks. How much your help has meant to me. I…"

He pulled her hands free and held them in his, rubbing her knuckles as he said, "I don't know what's happened to me since I came home this morning, but I can hold Beth and…and it's almost like it was before."

"Almost?" Rolleen whispered.

Gavin let out a soughing sigh and met Rolleen's gaze. "I love her, I think. But she isn't...something's missing."

Rolleen pulled her hands free. Gavin had given a part of himself back to his child. But he wasn't willing to risk everything. Until he was, there was no hope for the two of them.

"You have to love Beth with your whole heart, Gavin."

"But Beth is not—"

"Daddy?"

Rolleen turned to find Beth standing by the couch, a baby bottle in one hand and the doll in the crook of her arm.

"Daddy?" she repeated, her tiny brow furrowed.

She watched as Gavin met his daughter's confused, wide-eyed stare and then turned to look at her. His agonized expression asked *What should I do?*

She only wants to be loved, Rolleen said with her eyes. *Blood isn't the only thing that makes you her father. She needs you, Gavin. Love her. Just love her.*

Gavin turned back to Beth and held his arms open wide. "Come to Daddy, Beth," he said. "And let me give you a Christmas hug."

Beth shot a hesitant look at Rolleen, whose eyes had brimmed with tears of joy. She nodded to the little girl, who leaped into her father's arms and held him tight, crying, "Daddy, Daddy!"

Rolleen was happy for Gavin, but more than ever aware that she didn't belong in this picture. She had risen to leave them alone, when Gavin said, "I love you, Rolleen. Stay with us."

The love in Gavin's eyes was unmistakable. Rolleen's knees were threatening to buckle and it would have been easier to drop back onto the couch than it was to leave. But there was too much at stake to take the easy way out.

"It isn't just me you have to love, Gavin," she reminded him. "There's someone else who needs to be considered." She put her hand on her belly and felt a fluttery kick inside. She looked down and stared. "Oh."

"What's wrong?" Gavin asked.

"I felt something. The baby," she said. She lifted her eyes and met his gaze. "My baby needs a father as much as Beth does. Are you willing to take on that kind of responsibility?"

"I think I can."

Rolleen felt like she was going to throw up—and not because of the baby. *I think I can* just wasn't good enough. *I think I can* didn't come close to a lifetime commitment to love her and the child she carried inside her.

"It's not enough," she said. "Not nearly enough."

She turned and headed for Gavin's bedroom. She was running before she'd taken too many steps.

"Rolleen!" he called after her. She heard him tell Beth, "You play with Mary, and I'll see you in a little while." Then she heard his boots on the hardwood floor chasing after her.

She ran down the hall searching for the room where he'd taken her before. But she lost her way and found herself in a feminine bedroom with a lace canopy over the bed and a white lace bedspread. She turned to slam the door and found Gavin blocking the doorway.

"Wait, Rolleen," he said. "Don't run away."

She couldn't keep him out, but she couldn't face him, either. Rolleen clambered onto the bed, grabbed a pillow and curled herself into a protective ball around it. "Go away!" she said. "As soon as I'm feeling better I want you to take me home."

She heard the door shut and Gavin's footsteps crossing slowly to the bed. She knew he was close when the steps became muffled by the rag rug beside it. She felt the bed sag as he lay down beside her, felt the heat of him as he scooted closer.

"I was wrong," he said, laying a soothing hand on her shoulder.

"What?"

He pulled her gently toward him, laying her flat so he was above her, looking down at her. "I said I was wrong. About myself. About my feelings."

"You don't have to say what you think I want to hear," Rolleen said.

"I'm not saying it because you want to hear it. I'm saying it because it's true. I love you, Rolleen. Which means I love everything that's a part of you. And this baby—" He laid his hand caressingly on her belly. "Is a part of you I'll always cherish—because it brought us together."

"Oh, Gavin." Rolleen couldn't see him clearly for the tears blurring her eyes. "I want to believe you."

He leaned down and kissed her belly. "Listen to me, you in there. This is your father speaking. I want you to stop making your mother sick, do you hear me? I want you to concentrate on growing so we can welcome you as part of the family." He met her gaze and said, "There. I'm already giving the kid 'what for.' Is that proof enough I'm ready to be his father?"

Rolleen gave a choked laugh. "You're ridiculous."

"I'm in love," Gavin said. "With you."

Rolleen met Gavin's gaze and saw nothing there but tenderness and yearning and desire. "I love you, too, Gavin."

"Will you marry me and have my baby?" he asked, his hand caressing her belly.

"Oh, Gavin," she said. "Oh, Gavin…"

"Will you be my wife, Rolleen? Will you be the mother of my children?"

Rolleen swallowed down the thickness in her throat and said. "Oh, yes, Gavin. Yes."

The door clicked open and Rolleen turned and saw a small face peeking in.

"What are you two doing?" Beth asked.

"Come here," Gavin said, extending a hand to her.

Moments later Beth and her doll were snuggled up between the two of them. "I like this," Beth said dreamily.

"Me, too," Gavin said. "How about if we ask Rolleen to hang around so we can do this all the time."

Beth eyed Rolleen and said, "Okay."

"I guess it's settled then," Gavin said as he gathered the two of them—the three of them, Rolleen mentally corrected—into his arms. "We're a family."

Rolleen met Gavin's eyes and smiled. "Merry Christmas, Gavin."

"Merry Christmas, Rolleen."

Beth snuggled close, gave a satisfied sigh and said, "And God bless Us, Every One!"

* * * * *

**Turn the Page for a
Special Holiday Interview
with Bestselling Author
Joan Johnston**

A Conversation with Joan Johnston

Q. How did you make the transition from attorney to romance author?

A. "I had just gone to work as an attorney for the largest law firm in Virginia and had a six-month-old and a six-year-old. The stress of trying to be Superwoman was overwhelming. I turned to romance novels for escape. In the novels the woman always won, no matter how difficult the obstacles in her way. Once I had read about a thousand novels—over three years—I decided to write one that ended the way I wanted it to end. I started writing on June 1, 1983, and I sold my first partial manuscript to the first editor I submitted it to on April 24, 1984 at 11:00 a.m. It's like the birth of your first baby. You never forget it."

Q. What is your favorite aspect of writing?

A. "I love being able to work on my own schedule. That means if I really want to do something during the week, I can work longer hours or over the weekend to compensate. I also love traveling to do research. I've been to Tahiti and Egypt, to Texas and Wyoming. It's a ball!"

Q. What does Christmas mean to you?

A. "Christmas is my favorite time of year. I always decorate the first weekend in December to make the holiday last longer. I put up as many lights as I can and always look forward to putting the decorations on the tree because each one reminds me of a past Christmas. I especially enjoy the candlelight service on Christmas Eve. You can feel the hope and joy and goodwill toward men all around you."

Q. Do you have a favorite holiday story from your childhood?

A. *Amahl and the Night Visitors*. It's really an operetta, but my family and I used to watch it on TV every Christmas. It's the story of a poor crippled shepherd boy who offers his crutch to the baby Jesus and is miraculously healed because of his selfless generosity. I think this must have been when I fell in love with happy endings."

Q. What is the best gift you ever received?

A. "Twenty-three years ago I spent Christmas day in the hospital and was rewarded with the best Christmas gift I ever received–my lovely daughter, Heather."

Q. Do you have any holiday tips to offer on how to buy the perfect present?

A. "I always ask my children to give me a list of what they'd like to have for Christmas. I don't always get them everything on the list. For instance, my seventeen-year-old son, Blake, asked for a Lamborghini last year. I got him a toy model instead, which was fun to shop for and fun for him to receive. I also pay attention to the things my kids use, and the things they say they wish they had. Believe me, they drop enough hints–if you're listening–to make Christmas shopping easy."

Q. What kinds of tree trimmings can we find around your home?

A. "My tree is trimmed and my house adorned with decorations my two children have made at school over the years. The paper-plate angel my daughter made in first grade still graces the top of our tree now that she's a college graduate. A glittery construction-paper Christmas tree and candy cane and a cotton ball-and-cork Santa my son made are wonderful decorations. When my son was seven, we bought a '#7' decoration that he painted himself and signed with his name. One year we bought an ornament to hold a picture and had a picture taken of the three of us."

Q. Do you practice any family holiday traditions?

A. "We always open our stocking gifts on Christmas Eve and attend the Christmas Eve candlelight service. We take turns opening presents on Christmas Day. This past Christmas my two kids and I started a new tradition of trying to put together a 500-piece puzzle on Christmas Eve. We got about a third done before the kids left to spend time with their father. My daughter's vizsla, a kind of weimaraner, but cinnamon-colored with yellow eyes, ate a puzzle piece, so I guess next year, if we manage to finish the puzzle, we'll find out which piece it was.

"In addition, each Christmas my children and I shop for two or three decorations to add to the tree. They are mementos of where we are. For instance, a 'Merry Kiss-Moose' from our winter in Wyoming. A cowboy boot and chili pepper from Texas. A skiing bunny from our Christmas in Vermont. And a Ninja Turtle decoration from the year they were my son's favorite toy."

Q. Do you have a holiday message for your readers?

A. "Christmas is all about families spending time together celebrating the birth of Jesus. I hope this Christmas you and your family find love and joy in the holiday season."

Joan Johnston

✝ ✝ ✝ ✝ ✝ ✝ ✝ ✝

TWICE-BAKED SWEET POTATOES

Joan's traditional Christmas dinner is ham, twice-baked sweet potatoes, asparagus and cranberry sauce.

4 large sweet potatoes
1/2 cup butter or margarine (use less if you're dieting)
1 cup grated colby cheddar cheese
  (or the cheddar of your choice)
5 slices crisply cooked bacon, crumbled
Salt to taste

Scrub potatoes, dry well. Prick skin with fork. Cook in 425°F oven for approximately one hour, or microwave on high for approximately 8 minutes per sweet potato, until tender.

Remove a thin horizontal slice from the top of the baked sweet potato. Gently scoop out inside of potato, leaving skin intact. Combine scooped-out sweet potatoes with butter, 3/4 cup of grated cheese, 4 slices of crumbled bacon and salt. Beat with a wooden spoon until fluffy. Use to refill sweet potato skins. Top each potato with remaining grated cheese and last slice of crumbled bacon. Return to oven for 15 minutes, or microwave for 2–2 1/2 minutes, or until cheese is melted. Serves 4.

PEANUT BLOSSOMS

Joan's children also love cookies and request peanut blossoms at Christmas because they mix two favorites–peanut butter and chocolate.

1/2 cup shortening
1/2 cup peanut butter
1/2 cup sugar
1/2 cup brown sugar
1 egg
2 tbsp milk
1 tbsp vanilla
1 3/4 cup flour
1 tsp baking soda
1/2 tsp salt
1 bag chocolate kisses, unwrapped

Mix together shortening, peanut butter, sugar and brown sugar. Add one unbeaten egg, milk and vanilla. Blend flour, soda, and salt, and then add to peanut butter mixture. Shape into balls and roll in sugar. Bake on ungreased cookie sheet at 350°F for 8 minutes. Remove cookies from oven and press one milk chocolate kiss into each cookie making it look cracked. Return to oven and bake for 2 minutes. Makes 4 dozen cookies.

FIVE UNIQUE SERIES
FOR EVERY WOMAN YOU ARE...

♥ *Silhouette* ROMANCE™

From classic love stories to romantic comedies to emotional heart tuggers, Silhouette Romance is sometimes sweet, sometimes sassy—and always enjoyable! Romance—the way you always knew it could be.

SILHOUETTE® *Desire*®

Red-hot is what we've got! Sparkling, scintillating, *sensuous* love stories. Once you pick up one you won't be able to put it down...only in Silhouette Desire.

Silhouette® SPECIAL EDITION®

Stories of love and life, these powerful novels are tales that you can identify with—romances with "something special" added in! Silhouette Special Edition is entertainment for the heart.

SILHOUETTE·INTIMATE·MOMENTS®

Enter a world where passions run hot and excitement is always high. Dramatic, larger than life and always compelling—Silhouette Intimate Moments provides captivating romance to cherish forever.

♥ SILHOUETTE YOURS TRULY™

A personal ad, a "Dear John" letter, a wedding invitation... Just a few of the ways that written communication unexpectedly leads Miss Unmarried to Mr. "I Do" in Yours Truly novels...in the most fun, fast-paced and flirtatious style!

CHRISTMAS MIRACLES

**really can happen, and Christmas
dreams can come true!**

BETTY NEELS,
Carole Mortimer and Rebecca Winters

bring you the magic of Christmas in this wonderful
holiday collection of romantic stories intertwined
with Christmas dreams come true.

Join three of your favorite romance authors as they
celebrate the festive season in their own special style!

Available in November at your favorite retail store.

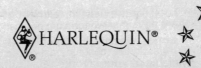

HARLEQUIN®

Look us up on-line at: http://www.romance.net   CMIR

Welcome to the Towers!

In January
New York Times bestselling author

NORA ROBERTS

takes us to the fabulous Maine coast mansion
haunted by a generations-old secret and introduces
us to the fascinating family that lives there.

Mechanic Catherine "C.C." Calhoun and hotel magnate
Trenton St. James mix like axle grease and mineral
water—until they kiss. Efficient Amanda Calhoun finds
easygoing Sloan O'Riley insufferable—and irresistible.
And they all must race to solve the mystery
surrounding a priceless hidden emerald necklace.

Catherine and Amanda

THE Calhoun Women

**A special 2-in-1 edition containing
COURTING CATHERINE and A MAN FOR AMANDA.**

Look for the next installment of
THE CALHOUN WOMEN with Lilah and Suzanna's
stories, coming in March 1998.

Available at your favorite retail outlet.

Return to the Towers!

In March
New York Times bestselling author

NORA ROBERTS

brings us to the Calhouns' fabulous
Maine coast mansion and reveals the
tragic secrets hidden there for generations.

For all his degrees, Professor Max Quartermain has a
lot to learn about love—and luscious Lilah Calhoun is
just the woman to teach him. Ex-cop Holt Bradford is
as prickly as a thornbush—until Suzanna Calhoun's
special touch makes love blossom in his heart.
And all of them are caught in the race to solve
the generations-old mystery of a priceless
lost necklace…and a timeless love.

Lilah and Suzanna
THE
Calhoun Women

**A special 2-in-1 edition containing
FOR THE LOVE OF LILAH and
SUZANNA'S SURRENDER**

Available at your favorite retail outlet.

Daniel MacGregor is at it again...

New York Times bestselling author

NORA ROBERTS

introduces us to a new generation of MacGregors
as the lovable patriarch of the illustrious MacGregor
clan plays matchmaker again, this time to his three
gorgeous granddaughters in

THE MACGREGOR BRIDES

From Silhouette Books

Don't miss this brand-new continuation of Nora Roberts's
enormously popular *MacGregor* miniseries.

Available November 1997 at your favorite retail outlet.

Look us up on-line at: http://www.romance.net   NRMB-S

WELCOME TO *Love Inspired* ™

A brand-new series of contemporary inspirational love stories.

Join men and women as they learn valuable lessons about facing the challenges of today's world and about life, love and faith.

Look for:

Promises
by Roger Elwood

A Will and a Wedding
by Lois Richer

An Old-Fashioned Love
by Arlene James

Available in retail outlets
in October 1997.

LIFT YOUR SPIRITS AND GLADDEN YOUR HEART with *Love Inspired* ™!

Steeple
Hill™

LI1197